Praise for a Gray New Deal:

"In this deeply original novel of communal living, a group of seniors move back into the college co-op where they once came of age. What starts as a nostalgic experiment becomes a moving exploration of grief, love, friendship, memory, and the unfinished work of growing older, reminding us what it means to be alive at any age."
— Chaitali Sen, author of *The Pathless Sky* and *A New Race of Men from Heaven*

"Miriam Kuznets finely wrought and deeply felt debut, *The Grey New Deal*, is a paean to the hope that one can choose one's own family. The cast of this wry and often funny novel were housemates back in college; time, fate, a lack of funds, and everlasting attachment have brought them back to living in a co-op of sorts where they annoy, enhance and stand by one another through the buffeting winds of these crazy times. Their stories are pure, contemporary Americana."
— Helen Schulman, author of *Fools for Love* and *Lucky Dogs*

"*The Gray New Deal* is a hymn to precarity. The friends of West House, aging and downwardly mobile, are brought together at first by necessity, drifting through a precisely realized Texas hovering on the edge of the COVID pandemic. This is a book about the small and slow and necessary actions that create community, and as its characters reckon with the wounds of the past and the uncertainty of their future, they show us how fragility can be transformed into strength."
— Celia Bell, author of *The Disenchantment*

"Elegant and profoundly funny, *The Gray New Deal* reads like a timeless parable about connection and community. But as her characters risk loving each other in a world where disruption—a geological outburst, a nasty lockdown—has become the norm, we realize that Miriam Kuznets has lured us through the looking-glass. We end up gazing with astonished eyes at the strange world we live in now."—Debra Jo Immergut, author of *You Again* and *The Captives*

"Miriam Kuznets has written a brilliant novel that preserves in amber the absurd times we are living through. It opens with a powerful image that brings to mind the toxic event of Don DeLillo's *White Noise*, but it's presented with the empathy and warmth of Elizabeth Strout's *Olive Kitteridge*. Throughout, Kuznets's sentences perform a sleight-of-hand that only the best writers achieve, simultaneously drawing me into the novel's many worlds while causing me to pause long enough to appreciate the beauty of the writing. I flat-out love this book, and I urge you to read it."—John McNally, author of *The Book of Ralph* and *The Fear of Everything*

"The intimacy of the characters' lives in *The New Gray Deal* feels utterly compelling and impossible to turn away from. Miriam Kuznets has written an endearing novel that brims with compassion and healing, two things the world could use more of these days."—Oscar Cásares, author of *Where We Come From*

THE GRAY NEW DEAL

A novel by
Miriam Kuznets

Flexible Press
Minneapolis, Minnesota, 2026

COPYRIGHT © 2026 Miriam Kuznets
All Rights Reserved. This is a work of fiction.
Names, characters, places, and incidents are the products of the
author's imagination, and any resemblance to an actual person,
living or dead, events, or locales is entirely coincidental.

Print ISBN: 979-8-9998771-3-0
eBook ISBN: 979-8-9998771-4-7

Flexible Press LLC
Minneapolis, Minnesota
www.flexiblepub.com
Editors William E Burleson
Vicki Adang, Mark My Words Editorial Services, LLC
Cover William Burleson, photos via Canva

To Max and Eli Taub,
my greatest delights.

The Gray
New Deal

Chapter 1: Infrastructure

A FEW MONTHS after settling in, the group strolls down their cul-de-sac and stares into the growing hole in the street, which they had first assumed was just a pothole. It's now an underground cauldron of oily iridescent water topped with a solo gray sock. "How's that still floating?" asks Pearl, but no one ventures a guess. She is someone who nods a lot, so she does that, even though her friends aren't piping up. The sock's potential for buoyancy must be vaster than she'd imagined, a surprising possibility in line with all the shocking turns she and the globe keep taking.

Jane, the retired veterinarian, wears birding binoculars hung around her neck, and as she squints in search of the hole's bottom, her hands shake. The street's erosion reminds Jane of one of her own disintegrations: Essential hand tremors have sabotaged her ability to work. Beta blockers, Botox injections, occupational therapy—she'd spent half her savings to no avail. Still, that was nothing in comparison to what happened to her daughter. Don't think about Amy, she tells herself. As if to comfort Jane, a marmalade tabby from the street's semi-feral colony approaches her and swirls around her legs. "Ginger Rogers," she says, her hand steady when atop the cat's back. But the dim hole is malignant, no longer a normal blemish on the street's skin. The pit seems larger, discolored, with irregular borders.

Vihaan says, "I think the damn thing's getting bigger." As usual, he looks spiffy in his tennis whites, ready for a match. He paces the hole's circumference, wonders why an elusive someone hasn't fixed the mess.

"Should we move the Odyssey?" asks Tomás, perspiring from his after-dinner cleanup shift. The group has a big white Honda with room for all of them.

"Couldn't hurt to have an escape vehicle," says Ellen in her crimson robe. Though it's almost her early-bird bedtime, the gaping cavity in the street makes her too anxious to consider sleep. From afar, she still resembles a Modigliani subject, a big draw when Tomás was getting his MFA and Ellen had been in his section of Painting 101, back when a teacher pursuing a student had been par for the course.

After the housemates move the car to the block outside West Circle, the hole's edges seem to distend. Surely the hole is bigger than it was a few minutes ago. Pearl and Doris link arms and volunteer to warn Neighbor David about the development. David's home office overlooks the cul-de-sac, so he saw what happened to the last tenant of the group's house. He told the group about it over brunch last week at their long table. Facing eviction after a twofold rent increase, the woman who'd lived there left houseplants on the driveway with a sign that said "Free" before setting herself and her sofa on fire. When David smelled smoke, and the tenant staggered out to collapse near the potted cacti, he called 911. The woman survived, but David read in the news that she was serving a long sentence for arson.

The night after Doris heard the story, her restless legs thrashed as she imagined the woman's agony. Doris had fled her San Diego bungalow when the 2017 fires had roared through.

Now making their way to Neighbor David, Doris and Pearl pass an empty house in foreclosure and, on a smaller lot, the long-standing skeleton of a spec McMansion. The marinara from the spaghetti dinner she'd fixed for dinner-duty sizzles in Pearl's gut. She reattaches the elastic on her long braid.

The hole is gaping further. They should have measured it, but Vihaan guesses it's half a foot bigger than it was earlier. "What the hell?" he says. "Should we stay here?"

The chorus says, "Why not?" and Vihaan shrugs. A former tennis pro, he's the most able-bodied, and he tucks under his arm several webbed aluminum folding chairs from their backyard and unfolds them a safe distance from the hole. Barry, Jane, Tomás, and Doris each carry a seat to the viewing section. At the same time, Ellen fetches a family-size bag of marshmallows, offering to her left and passing to the right, an etiquette school remnant.

Barry gestures to the street and says, "There goes the neighborhood." The neighborhood is already metaphorically half-gone, their nearby alma mater rocked by harassment and embezzlement scandals, exploitation of adjuncts, and mold-filled buildings.

Tomás googles "collapse street surface." In the past few months, he's called the city twenty-seven times to repair the street, but no one has responded. He leaves another message in the city's baroque system.

Trailing Pearl and Doris, Neighbor David strolls across his gravel lawn to join the group.

"Welcome," says Barry.

Barry's huge moneymaker was Manhattan's Quilted Pig with the Michelin star that it's held for years. Why he wanted to remodel the group's old university co-op in the middle of climate-torn Texas (but where on earth wasn't?) and why he appreciates their communal econo-meals bewilders those who ponder the questions. Each of them is contributing to the household on a sliding scale. Jane concludes that Barry cares more about being surrounded by old friends than having a dwelling with more elbow room. Vihaan and Ellen imagine Barry might have a charity in mind for his money at some point, or maybe he'll swoop in and subsidize the rest of them even further when they need it more. Doris wonders if Barry still carries a torch for Tomás and Ellen, his ménage à trois back in the day. Pearl remembers Barry telling them about growing up in a homeless family. He'd undercut the sadness of being too starved to focus on schoolwork with a great Scarlett O'Hara impression: "I'll never go hungry again." Barry knew his friends were in danger of outliving their means.

The elders scoot outward to envelop Neighbor David, a fortysomething man with foggy glasses, as he perches on the curb.

"What would you want to throw into this hole if you could?" Doris asks the group.

"Something tangible?" Jane asks.

Doris loves that Jane is always game for whatever.

The group agrees to go back to their house for things to feed the hole. "Be right back," Barry assures David.

Doris calls out, "Whatever you throw in has to be compostable!"

Thuds and siftings later, they reconvene.

"I'll go first," Doris says. When the evacuation order had come in San Diego, she was already in the middle of a long, grief-driven sheltering in place. In the smudged mirror, she'd noted her inches of greasy white roots in unfashionable contrast to the hennaed auburn, and she registered her mouth, crusty and chapped. The shirt she'd worn for days had holes that weren't strategic. The wildfire had started not long after the living nightmare in which Doris's husband, Howard, had died of viral pneumonia. Doris strongly considered defying the wildfire evacuation, allowing the fire to be her funeral pyre. Instead, she'd forced herself to call friends in Los Angeles who had a guestroom.

"I'd put the destructive kind of fire down the hole to burn the crappy virus that killed my husband," Doris says with the customer-service tone she retains. She hauls herself out of her chair and clutches an old cigar box as she grapevines toward the hole.

Miming lifting an enormous weight from the ground, straining, her arms outstretched and aching, she heaves the imaginary load of the box. In it are ashes she scooped up from the site of her collapsed house, and she pours a gray waterfall of them into the hole. "Be gone!" She wipes her hands on her slacks and grapevines back to the applauding friends. She and Howard had met through folk dancing. Though she can only lower herself a few inches without her knees giving out, she curtsies and asks, "Who's next?" By focusing on this ritual, she tamps down the part of her that just wants to take the group's Odyssey and head somewhere far away. But where? Besides, she never renewed her driver's license.

Jane raises her hand, peels Ginger Rogers from her lap, and stands. "I'd bury Amy's pain." She looks at Neighbor David. "She was my daughter."

He gives a solemn nod, wondering what he's getting into with this group. His ex had complained that his first response to an invitation was no, and he'd been stretching to grow what she called "yes-siness." Maybe this is too much of a stretch.

Jane hugs herself and closes her eyes. Barry, next to her, takes her hand. Back when Jane had been in her thirties, a friend banked his sperm for her. She hid the insemination from her girlfriend, who ditched her when it became obvious. The night after the girlfriend had stormed out, she'd returned to Jane's house to snip off the heads of every rose in the garden. After her daughter died, Jane wondered if the girlfriend's outrage had trickled down to Amy in the womb. Her head knew Amy's perfect storm had countless causes, but her heart so longed for a clearer cause and effect.

Jane approaches the hole and bows her heavy head as if this were a hole into which Amy's friends lowered her corpse. Riddled with panic attacks, Amy had flunked out of MIT. She first tasted Oxy after she broke her femur skiing, joking with friends about a slippery slope on the few occasions she admitted she had a problem. When she died, Amy had no friends left, and Jane had her cremated.

She digs in her pocket and unearths a dried rose from the bushes that had refused to give up the ghost at her old house, and now she lets the rose float into the hole. Back in the semicircle, Jane free-falls the last couple of inches into her chair, and Ginger snuggles up. "Good kitty," Jane whispers.

Ellen's eyes water at the thought of losing her own son and daughter, while Tomás regrets not having reached out more to Jane when she lost Amy. Vihaan and the others look glassy-eyed. Vihaan thinks about the DUI ticket his son, Will, got and how Vihaan had shouted at him, "You're so careless!" Since then, all his son seems to want from him is the money that Vihaan no longer has.

"Love you, Jane," Barry is saying. "Always." After Amy died, he FaceTimed Jane on Monday evenings, offering tissues she couldn't reach through the screen. He'd shipped her a care package every month—pears, a new novel, an azure blouse with no pesky buttons.

Sunset is painting the mackerel sky a rich salmon. The light in West Circle is shining from a Moonlight Tower, a white whale of a streetlight that had been built in the 1890s to prevent nighttime crime after the "servant girl annihilator" terrorized the city, or so the tale went.

Barry rises to his feet. "I'd pitch in that hole my Achilles heel—settling for love crumbs. And I don't mean you guys," he says to the group, his eyes lingering on Ellen and Tomás, both of whom look startled. For a short, solidly built man, Barry's strides are long and graceful. He sees the wavery reflection of his shiny bald head in the street hole's brew, and he imagines his heart filtering out all the times he had been his first choice's second or third or umpteenth choice. The last entanglement had been with a fellow occupant of the Manhattan condo building where Barry lived for so long, a few blocks from the Quilted Pig. That delectable man and Barry had first chatted in the elevator, where the man's scent of five-spice and the rumble of his voice hypnotized Barry. When the man's husband was away, with Barry he'd played. For hours and hours, they'd strolled the city, stopping to hold hands under happy hour tables where they shared cocktails with ingredients like pork-fat washed never-sink gin and Cimarron Blanco Tequila. Their time together had dried up with the man's excuses, and Barry had begun to dread running into the man on the elevator so much that he took the stairs up and down from his eighth-floor sanctuary with its luxuriant sectional sofa and view of the Hudson. He'd consoled himself by thinking that the extra stair-climbing was strengthening his shredded heart.

To spit into the pothole would be disrespectful, especially after Doris and Jane have left their tragedies in there, so Barry tosses in a cocktail napkin on which he and his old flame had written affectionate words. He waves goodbye to the murky water and returns to his friends.

Ellen raises her hand. "I'll take a turn." After she smooths her robe, she looks at her husband, Tomás. Vihaan tenses because Ellen and Tomás together have an air of drama, an unpleasant intensity. He likes each of them more when the other is elsewhere. She says, "To the times I've hurt you. To how I've hurt myself." Tomás's response is to swallow, his Adam's apple huge.

Vihaan and Doris exchange exasperated glances, and Barry wonders if Neighbor David wants to flee from this confessional. David examines a blade of grass. It's impressive and embarrassing that the group is so open. Barry wants to take care of David's feelings, though he knows David is an adult.

Ellen steeples her elegant fingers together. She'd moved back to the new old co-op to stop her affairs, to eat more than nine hundred calories a day, and to revive the painting she backburnered during her decades as a relentless real estate agent. Ellen's last sex buddy had died of a heart attack on the toilet of the staged house in Dallas where they were rendezvousing. The paramedics declared him dead, and Ellen escaped from the scene as soon as possible. At least the man had been dressed to go back to work, but Ellen's discovery of him slumped over still haunts her. She'd had the decency to call the man's wife from the hospital.

When Ellen had unraveled the truth about her infidelities to Tomás, they didn't know if their marriage could survive, and they still don't. Still, Ellen is relishing food these days and imagining her bones strengthening from the greater nourishment. The walls of Tomás's and her bedroom are showcasing her new paintings, while her housemates clamor for her to create a masterpiece for the living room. Now and then, she pictures Barry naked and touching her—he's so different from Tomás—but the fantasies float out of sight when given time.

From the pocket of her robe, Ellen takes a short stack of her old business cards to the hole and stands at its craggy edge. A fear of falling, slipping into the hole, washes over her. What if she jumps in? She leans back, unsteady. The others brace for a rescue. She hurls the cards into the hole as if they were a weapon to surprise the slimy creature that could leap out of the hole and suffocate her. The cards fan out and float, paper water lilies.

Ellen returns to the fold and sees that Tomás, her friends, and even the neighbor look at her with what feels like warmth. Well, Vihaan is more neutral than friendly-looking, but that's Vihaan. Jane passes her the bag of marshmallows, and Ellen sinks her fingers into it before plucking one out and letting its lightness rest on her tongue.

"I'll take a turn," Pearl says. She wears her salt-and-pepper hair in a braid that reaches the middle of her back. Today, her capris are lemon yellow, her blouse lavender, and she stands in front of her friends the way she stood in front of the kids during storytime at the Flint Public Library. "As most of you know, I was in Flint during the first water crisis, and I'd throw that in the stinking hole." As a librarian here in Austin, Pearl shares classics like *Bread and Jam for Frances, My Aunt Came Back,* and *The Snowy Day,* while keeping up with newer gems. After the Flint water crisis started, her sleep teemed with children drowning in a carnivorous ocean, no shores in sight. She'd forgotten how to swim. In one nightmare, finally, she'd grasped a boy, but he'd dissolved to rust and crumbled in her arms.

While Pearl knows that most drinking water she encounters is safe enough now, she skirts her skepticism by saying a silent thank you every time clean water flows into her midnight-blue mug. In the hole, the water recedes, as if the well had just deepened another level. Pearl tips her empty mug and pretends to pour water into her cupped hand. To allow the invisible water to escape into the pit, she spreads her fingers. She nods yes as she recalls the free improv class back in college, during which she and Doris had irritated the teacher by cracking up midsentence, interrupting the sacred riffing.

"Thank you, Pearlie," says Vihaan as he bounces on the balls of his feet.

She nods yes. Did she nod so much when they were young?

He twirls a tennis racket into the air and catches it as if it were a baton. "I can go next. I'm going to disappear cancer. And bullying." He and his family were the only people of Hindu descent in the rural town in which he grew up. "Grubby!" the boys would chant at him on the playground as the schoolyard guardians turned a blind eye. When he threw a pebble at one of the boys, it was Vihaan's mother who was called to get him from the principal's office.

When Vihaan had attended the university, he'd dated Anglo women who complimented him on the "richness" of his skin, and he straddled an uneasy edge between feeling appreciated and feeling exoticized. He'd found a kindred spirit in his wife, Rose, a Black woman who also felt isolated in her small hometown, and they'd celebrated their golden anniversary before she died of breast cancer in 2016 just after the election.

His neck aches as he strolls over to the hole. The memories feel so present—betrayed by the carelessness of the schoolyard bullies, betraying his son by his lack of patience, betraying his wife when he made excuses to be away from home as she lay in her sickbed. "Behold," he says. "Excelsior!" He holds up a tennis ball, a prototype biodegradable one he developed, one of his get-rich-again schemes.

The street hole creaks, and Vihaan raises his racket to smash the ball of shame into it.

"Your advantage, Vihaan!" says Doris.

Tomás points his chin at the hole. "It's getting bigger." The asphalt around the hole has fissures, growing cracks. The other group members are unsure whether the hole is indeed bigger or it's just their imagination. He had cataract surgery before the move into the house and is delighted by the resulting clarity. "Well, I'll take a turn before we get swallowed up." He clears his throat. "I'm trying to quit my two-dimensional ways of seeing people." He gives a subtle nod to Ellen and one to Barry. "Some of you know that I'm exploring the third dimension." He used to be a painter, but now, using gray egg cartons, he's constructing an elaborate homage to Gaudi's Sagrada Familia.

Vihaan tells himself to be generous with Ellen and Tomás to resist rolling his eyes.

On the way to the hole's edge, Tomás rubs the bracelet Ellen made him. That and running a hand over the texture of his shaved head serve as security blankets. "¡Vete con viento fresco!" He releases an origami tiger he'd made into the hole.

"Good riddance," David translates.

"Neighbor David," Jane says. Davi means beloved, as does Amy." "Would you like to throw something down the hole?"

David prefers the focus to be on someone or something besides himself. Yet his throat aches with envy and admiration of the way these neighbors open up. He stands. "I'm going to banish a fear or two. Ha!" He blushes. Into the hole he pitches a banana peel and an apple core. "Maybe a New Year's-in-May resolution. Toward that end, may I use your lawn?"

Pearl says, "Go for it."

David jogs to the eight-by-ten rug of prairie grass in the front yard of the house they call West House, as it was called in its earlier incarnation. After a couple of burpee exercises, he touches his toes and stretches his hamstrings. He places his glasses on the sidewalk. He performs an awkward cartwheel. It's been so long since he tried one that he barely manages to avoid flopping onto his bottom.

Tomás edges up to the hole that calls him with its groan and deepest sigh. He contemplates dialing 311.

David cartwheels. He's a bit dizzy, but he likes the feel of his blood rushing to his face, the lightness mixed with tension. His push-off hand is red, and so is his face. The seniors clap, and he laughs. Surely, it's not too late to make a family of friends. He wants to convince himself that it's a risk worth taking.

"Bravo!" says Vihaan. He wonders if David plays tennis.

At the sound from the hole, a grinding like that of a car crash none of them can see, David leaps away.

"Oh, shit!" Barry shouts.

The hole sucks in asphalt and is spreading so fast now that it's nearly the width of the street.

Tomás's stiff fingers manage the 911.

The more agile ones herd the others toward the cul-de-sac's entrance. The sinkhole—it's a sinkhole—crunches on bites of the sidewalk, and the air smells like burning plastic and sulfur.

People die, Doris tells herself as she heads toward the Odyssey. Screw having a license but having no car key is a deal-breaker. She heads back to Pearl and the rest of the group.

A siren wailing nearby drowns out the now-whisper of the hole.

After she exhales, Jane asks, "Is the monster just holding its breath?"

"Please don't anybody have a heart attack. Please," Barry says, feeling in danger of one himself. "I'm going to run and get the essentials. What do we need?"

Jane says, "Fred." Amy's ancient tuxedo cat. "I'm coming."

"Medicine," says Doris as she flashes back to the standstill on the Pacific Coast Highway as she fled the wildfire.

Ellen says, "Phones." She can make other paintings.

"Photos," says Vihaan. "I'll go with you."

"Me too," says Doris.

The marinara rises in Pearl's throat, and she chokes it back down. "Be careful," she urges the others in a loving, useless command.

Pearl wonders why they're taking so long. She paces, trying to distract herself from the waiting and from her heartburn. Finally, Barry, Vihaan, and Doris return with Fred in his carrier and with rolling suitcases stuffed with necessities. David emerges from his house with a family-size bag of dry cat food and pours it into the cat colony's kibble feeder.

A fire truck screeches to a halt, and firefighters pour out. "A sinkhole," the leader announces. "Lucky it didn't swallow your houses."

The fire crew shuts off the water to West Circle and arranges a necklace of orange cones around the sinkhole.

"Thank you, thank you," Barry says.

"We've seen a lot of sinkholes lately." One of the fire crew asks David's retreating back, "Hey, whatever happened to your neighbor, the woman we rescued?"

Before they'd moved back to Austin, over FaceTime, Barry showed his old co-op roommates West House's fenced-in backyard where their mascot, a grand live oak, still stood as a reassuring though untended touchstone. "Take a chance while we're in good enough shape," he said, his eyes brimming "We have a history." It was true. This subset of college co-opers kept in magnificent touch, for fifty years now and especially since the Trump election, thanks to Barry, their connector. Sometimes they called him "Greg," short for "gregarious."

The others agreed to Barry's daunting but more than generous invite, so he salvaged West House's exterior with cornflower blue Hardie plank, and inside he soundproofed walls for each individual and the couple to have a compact room. The new-old housemates minimized their belongings in their respective cities before their pilgrimages back to what would once again become home.

The group drives to David's ex-girlfriend's tent in an abandoned lot, and they watch as she welcomes him. He waves goodbye to the group. He and his ex duck their heads and disappear into the tent.

Barry suggests, "The Extended Stay hotel. My treat." Five of the others mumble thank-yous and we-owe-yous, while Ellen snores delicately.

The city engineers promise the sinkhole has spent itself, and the street department crams it full of concrete, sand, and asphalt.

The group discusses whether it's safe to return to West Circle.

"What's the alternative?" asks Jane.

Doris's dazed expression reminds Jane how baby Amy went limp in nonviolent protest when Jane approached with a fresh diaper.

They know they have nowhere else to go.

The weekend of their return to West House, the group invites David to a happy hour. They lug garden chairs to the street again and place them atop the center of the patched hole as if daring the ground to break again. Vihaan unfolds a card table for the refreshments. Barry folds napkins into roses and contributes a platter of his tomato crostini and Swiss chard tartlets. Ellen carries out the pitcher of ginger margaritas, while Tomás adds bottles of Italian soda for himself and the other teetotalers.

The crisis averted leaves them with an acute case of carpe diem, though they'll need to economize again soon. "To us," Barry says in a toast. "Safe enough for now."

"To taking back the night," Pearl says.

After the group goes back inside, David practices his cartwheel in the middle of the street, then presses his ear to the warm street scars to see what he can hear.

A year has passed since what the friends dubbed the Great Sinkhole.

To add credit to the household expense account, Doris hocks her wedding ring. She remembers first seeing Howard at those weekly folk dances—his grace, his abundant laughter, the simple charm of him passing cups of cold water to the dancers during the break. Before Howard, she'd thought she'd never marry, focusing instead on her job, her friends, and taking care of her parents. Doris had introduced Howard to the canyons, where he knew the Latin names of the flora, and he introduced her to his kids and their kids, to his decades-long book club. Every Saturday, they hosted the kids and grandkids for breakfast.

Doris picks up the phone to call her stepson.

Jane relaxes in the backyard under the mascot oak, holding Ginger Rogers. As she closes her eyes, she sees her Amy. They'd been snowed in one Thanksgiving during which Amy seemed her old clearheaded self. In the living room, they danced with flailing arms to songs Amy had played ad nauseam when she was a kid—Pink's "Get This Party Started" and OutKast's "Hey Ya." One dinner consisted of the cookies they had baked as much for the wafting scent as for the taste. Each night they played rounds of gin rummy before sprawling on the faded denim sofa to watch comedies. With the lightest touch, they held hands until they dozed off past midnight, Fred the Cat a warm cap for Amy.

Barry lies in bed, lulled by waves of a white noise app. Thoughts of his last love make him feel sexy, the memories now light enough, honey cutting vinegar in a tangy shrub drink.

At the library where Pearl works for a pittance, she pauses at the drinking fountain. In Flint, she hocked her first editions to contribute to the Water Mobile, which delivered to the doorsteps of folks who couldn't make it to the water distribution centers or carry the heavy bottles. They did what they could. She nods, yes, yes, yes.

With Sharpies, Ellen creates a patchwork of herself and Tomás as they've evolved. It hurts to depict her thinnest self, her masked self. Tomás wears sunglasses in many of Ellen's depictions, but in the center of the piece, what Ellen sees as the present, his naked eyes and laugh lines shine silver and black as the two of them face each other.

To the egg carton spires of his Sagrada Familia, Tomás affixes fall leaves on which he painted cameos of the co-op friends. Peering through his reading glasses, he pinches the thinnest paintbrush, concentration causing the tip of his tongue to overlap his bottom lip. The leaves' veins and midribs give his housemates subtle heft.

Vihaan plays Neighbor David in their weekly game at the dilapidated tennis court. The thwack of the ball shatters another expanse of the flimsy wall inside Vihaan, and in flows his family's lives, the stubborn love they exchanged. His wife, Rose, was an emotional athlete, and he asks for her guidance to connect to his son, and simply to connect.

Neighbor David wonders how the hell this man twice his age can book it across the court and whup that ball. By inviting his neighbors, his ex, and other folks for simple companionship, he's growing his social security. With these friends, he dips his toe into revealing what he used to hide even from himself, and he holds dear his friends' paved-over depths, their gritty, leap-of-faith hearts.

Chapter 2: Holding On

Pearl is the first of the group to share Tomás's and Ellen's bed. Minus Ellen, of course.

Ellen had spent one night on the thin sofa bed in the living room, and when she complained about her back but still didn't want to return to the bed she'd shared with Tomás, Pearl offered up her bed.

Pearl works at the nearby branch of the public library, Monday through Thursday, noon to six, Saturday, ten to three. Bedtime for Pearl is midnight, and she inches into the space Tomás left her. In the light radiating from her phone, she sees that he is curled on his side, facing the wall. The tender top of his shaved head and his silver braceleted wrist are the only parts of him not covered by the vintage Marimekko quilt.

The last time she'd shared a bed with anyone was with her ex thirty years ago. During the too long period when they'd attempted to remain friends, when they'd tried to outrun the flood of mourning, they drove to the Detroit airport on MLK Friday and took the first flight to a warm place. Two nights on the beach, sand gritting the sheets, the salt taste of his mouth in the waves, the salt of her tears as he slept. She'd shaken the bed until her ex woke up, and then she pretended to be asleep. They had been under the illusion that you can say goodbye by making love. Back in Detroit, she ended up telling him she didn't want to talk with him anymore, and to her dismay, he'd respected her wish, probably his too.

Pearl remembers when Tomás had hair, a glossy black mop top, and back then she'd had to resist reaching out to run her fingers through it. Her room in the college co-op had been next to Ellen and Tomás's, and she'd blocked out their noise with a rattling box fan and the crackly hum created by tuning between radio stations.

Tomás still calls her "Perla."

She considers shaking the bed but not pretending to be asleep, and she imagines folding her hand, with its arthritic swellings, on top of his gnarled fingers. She wants them to converse sotto voce, and she wants to hear about what he and Ellen have really been up to these past fifty years, what his greatest joys, his fears, his sorrows have been. It's a tall order, she knows, nodding to herself to confirm it.

When Pearl and Tomás had talked at the co-op reunions and since sharing West House again, he has focused on her with such furrow-browed determination that he skirted the spotlight.

In this velvety brown near-dark, she could persist: "Let's talk about you." But that would be too intrusive. She places a finger on Tomás's scalp but feels almost nothing. Her hands have grown insensitive to temperature and texture, as if her fingertips have been sanded down. Her fingerprint doesn't even register anymore to unlock her phone, so she pecks in the password, bkwmn2. She yearns for the salt of her old boyfriend's mouth. Chin moving up and down, she nods herself to sleep.

Tomás is awake and appreciates Pearl's warm finger on his scalp. He'd thought he and Ellen were solid, and now here they are dragging the others into their drama.

"Can't you just pretend I'm not here?" Tomás had asked Ellen.

"I've tried, and it's not working. I can't sleep."

Did she dislike him so much? Hadn't his forgiveness of her affairs been enough to mend their rifts? He should have been the aggrieved and ambivalent one. Of course, she'd complained back when he'd been drinking, but that wasn't the same as infidelity, right?

This week she told him she'd considered escaping by visiting the kids, but they don't have the money for her to travel, and her relationship with the kids is strained anyway.

When Pearl awakes, the other half of the bed is still warm, but Tomás has left the room. She hoists herself to swing her legs over the side of the bed, and she sits there and counts, "One Mississippi" to ten. On several occasions, she's stood up too quickly and crumpled to the floor from low blood pressure.

When she was younger and had periods of gnawing depression, putting a sock on her bunioned foot had been a Sisyphean task. Now she's more patient, sees the obstacles less as indictments of her character than as neutral tolls on the road. Her mantra has become, "What's the rush?"

She finds her housemates in the kitchen. This morning Doris has whipped up a bowl of scrambled eggs, crowded a plate high with whole wheat toast and another with orange slices. Doris, who pores over the ever-changing recommendations for brain health, believes eggs help keep at bay the Alzheimer's monster, the one that ate her parents.

At the breakfast table, Ellen looks up from the crossword puzzle. "Thank you, Pearlie," Ellen says. "Your room's quite comfortable. But how did you sleep?"

Pearl, Tomás, and the rest of the group freeze, perhaps suspecting that Ellen has asked a trick question.

"Well enough, thank you."

Amid slurps of tepid coffee and scrapes of chair legs, the group members exhale once more. Pearl smiles at the thought that by giving up her bed, she's fulfilled a new unwritten addition to the chore chart. She nods to Tomás shyly, as if they'd done something untoward.

The crinkled skin under his eyes looks bruised, indigo and gray, as he gives her a wan smile in return.

Vihaan clears his throat. "Ellen, would you like to take my room tonight? That is, if you'll have me, Tomás. I don't think I have anything communicable." While he's often irritated by how the couple flips from syrup to acid with each other, Vihaan wants to channel the compassion his wife, Rose, would have had for the couple if she were still alive.

Ellen and Tomás agree to this, and soon each of the rest of them volunteers to bed-swap.

"Pajama parties," Barry says.

More laundry, thinks Jane. She's on laundry duty this week, and it seems only right to clean the sheets between bed-hops.

"I'll help with the extra laundry," says Barry, almost reading her mind, his gift.

Before they moved back to West, Barry had helped Jane winnow keepsakes of Amy from a cluttered room into a single moving box. He took photos of the bulky items that Jane had been reluctant to let go and made a slim photo album.

Vihaan folds his uniform of tennis whites over the back of a chair in Tomás and Ellen's room.

Each dressed only in boxer briefs, Vihaan's white, Tomás's emerald, the two men sit with the headboard of the bed as their backrest and play another round of gin. "Want to talk about it?" Vihaan asks. Though the skin on his belly sags, he is proud of the flatness of his stomach. The other house members, except for Ellen, look as if they're carrying abdominal balloons.

In the belief that it's an unwise tactic to hold on to face cards, Tomás discards the queen of hearts. "Maybe we should have gone our separate ways a while ago." His eyes are moist, pupils shrinking in the light. "But I didn't want to."

When she was younger, Ellen thought many times about leaving him, but then she'd be the villain and their still-in-the-nest kids would have spent half their time in a place where she was unwelcome, door slammed shut. What enabled her to stay were the dalliances. They distracted her from the hunger pangs. She adhered to a severe diet as if the only alternative were her spending all day, every day, in a hammock devouring Pinwheel cookies and Fritos.

When a man she barely knew was inside her, her stomach quieted its protest. She made sure the men were all married to someone else. When the last guy had the fatal heart attack, she finally let go of rationalizing the affairs as harmless. Maybe that guy would have had a heart attack anyway, but maybe their sex play had pushed him over the edge. What a mess she'd made.

Ellen turns her attention to Vihaan's sheets and comforter, like his clothes, shining white, milky glowing in the darkness. The down pillow makes her nose run, but beggars can't be choosers. In her dream, warm, sticky blood from her ears coats the pillowcase. When she awakes with a gasp, the sheets are unstained but damp from her perspiration. No more blood was her reward when she limped into menopause in her fifties.

She gathers the sheets and her sweaty nightgown and stuffs them in the washer, which provides a groaning and beeping soundtrack through its cycle. Ellen wants to spare Jane's trembling hands from laundry duty. She can picture Jane's skin-and-bone forearms dark with those bruises that appear mysteriously and take so long to heal when you're older. As Ellen turns from the laundry closet, Tomás approaches with his own brimming laundry basket. How well and how little they know each other. Their shy eyes meet and retreat, and they dance to get out of each other's way.

Because she'll be sharing a bed with him tonight, Doris suggests offhandedly that Tomás join her for the Saturday night folk dance at the community center. To her surprise, he is willing and appears in the living room at 6:45 sporting an orange-and-white Hawaiian shirt, so different from his alternating navy and black T-shirts.

At the folk dance group, Doris introduces Tomás to the regulars. Without Ellen, Tomás meets new people. Without Ellen, Tomás goes dancing. Without Ellen, Tomás grapevines the hora, holding Doris's hand in one of his, and an old man's in the other. This old man next to Tomás is probably younger than Tomás.

"Bow to your partner, bow to your corner," says the caller.

Each Saturday folk dance brings Doris closer in memory and further in time from Howard. She'd met him after her parents' drawn-out deaths, when her body felt alive again. Before that, she'd actively pushed away romance—more trouble than it was worth—but why not walk to her car with this cheery fellow who seemed so comfortable with himself, why not go for late-night gingerbread pancakes with him. The last time they'd gone folk dancing before he died, he'd bounced and spun and held her tight and reeled her out.

Four days after the last folk dance, Doris's sweetheart was in the hospital with pneumonia and something that looked like tuberculosis. She had to wear a hazmat suit to be in his room. When his eyes were open, he seemed frightened, maybe not recognizing her. With the fluids the staff pumped into him, Howard's skin became unwrinkled, and he looked younger than he had when she'd first met him.

After he died, the tuberculosis test came back negative, but the autopsy revealed kidney cancer. He had said he didn't want to die slowly. Her head knew his death was a good one, but …

Doris snaps back to the present. At the break, she and Tomás hand around cups of chilled water. Then they dance again. The air conditioning can't compete with the radiating bodies.

Back home, Tomás waits in the living room while Doris changes into her sleep clothes. In bed, she snores, so he tries to roll her gently onto her side, but she flips onto her back again.

The dancing has revved him up, and he ends up in a chair in the backyard with Ginger Rogers as a blanket across his lap as he pictures bodysurfing at one of those beaches that serve as a screensaver. He hums because humming is supposed to make you feel less sad.

It's five in the morning, and Ellen twitches with restlessness. She dons her ruby robe and slippers and glides out the back door with a cup of English breakfast. When she sees Tomás in a chair, she retreats and stands in the doorway until her eyes readjust to the darkness and she can make her way to the dining table. She's glad for the lack of company.

Tomás awakes with a start. Where is he? He is stiff and can barely stand straight. His arms itch with mosquito bites, which he scratches until they bleed, a welcome smarting, like wasabi or jalapeño. How many scabs does a seventy-two-year-old develop over the course of his lifetime, he wonders.

Barry is the next sleepover guest. "No hanky-panky," Ellen says to Tomás in the hallway.

As if that were in the realm of possibility, Tomás thinks. As if she's entitled to dictate the rules.

After the last man whom he'd been with had ditched him, Barry had started wearing the same cologne the man wore—a smoky cinnamon scent. Perhaps Barry wouldn't have been as attracted to his paramour had the fellow been au naturel. Perhaps he wouldn't have been as attracted had the man been available.

Tomás had been unavailable when Ellen started bringing him home to the co-op way back when. Still, twenty-year-old Barry's bidar rang, and he took to knocking on Ellen's door bearing a bottle of wine or cream puffs he'd made at the restaurant where he worked to put himself through college as a philosophy major. There'd been nowhere to sit in Ellen's room but her bed, which she patted to welcome Barry. Barry rubbed Tomás's back while Tomás kneaded Ellen's shoulders, and their hands had drifted.

Their ménage persisted until graduation, when Barry's grad school was the CIA, the culinary institute in New York. At first, Ellen and Tomás were going to move there too, but Tomás found a teaching position in Dallas, and that was that.

Barry sniffs his wrist as he lies in bed waiting for Tomás to join him. As Tomás pulls the comforter off his side of the bed, Barry says, "Look behind your pillow."

"Tooth fairy?"

"Of sorts."

A confectioner's box with dark chocolate raspberry truffles. They each let one melt in their mouth, then another and another. Now they can sleep.

Ellen feels a lump under Barry's pillow. The blue of the box reminds Ellen of Tiffany's, but this box contains three truffles.

She squirrels one in each cheek and drifts off before they dissolve. Instead of grinding her teeth, she is chewing chocolate, breathing in the cologne-spiced Egyptian cotton of Barry's sheets.

In Barry's coat closet in his New York apartment, he'd had an emergency supply of smoked mussels, caviar, salmon jerky, cream crackers, and bottles of port. He was never far from a bounty of food. If he and Tomás and she had stayed together, where would they be now? Would she have become anorexic, or would Barry's company and food have liberated her?

It is enough to be in Barry's bed, one more truffle before morning. Chocolate is better, and easier these days, than anything else. So much time Ellen had wasted avoiding eating. She misses Tomás just a little bit. She no longer expects him to read her mind, to give her what she thinks she wants. Maybe his forgiveness is enough, and she wonders how she can be more forgiving.

Sheets passing in the hall again, and Tomás bows to Ellen.

He's at work on his Sagrada Familia when he hears Jane's gentle knock.

Jane and her tuxedo cat are tonight's guests in Tomás's room. The cat makes himself at home by swirling around the bed and landing on Ellen's pillow that is Jane's for tonight.

"What would you do differently if you had a do-over?" Jane asks. She still corners herself with this question when thinking of the daughter she lost. However, she doesn't want to talk about it. She still has some secrets.

Tomás realizes that if he had a do-over, he would have talked more openly with Ellen a long, long time ago, and he wouldn't have assumed he knew or understood her. He doesn't want to talk about it with Jane.

Yet he does assume that it's Ellen who's clearing her throat in the hallway outside their bedroom, and it's Ellen considering whether to come in and say a proper good night.

In the hall, Ellen raises her hand.

Chapter 3: Overtime

Jane uses the term "literally" with care. Still, she would describe herself as literally worried sick about Fred the Cat. He's been wasting away for a long time. Not having eaten anything at all for two days, Fred hides under the bed. His normal self would be following Jane from room to room and sitting near or on her, shedding. She's lost her appetite, and her throat feels like a firm hand is squeezing it.

As a retired vet, Jane knows it's time to say goodbye to Fred. He is twenty and half his top weight. Her knees won't allow her to get the cat from under the bed, so athletic Vihaan pulls Fred out gently. The cat tolerates her petting, but he isn't purring. As soon as she stops touching him, he crawls to the corner of the room, crouching, heaving, gasping for breath.

Vihaan drives them to the emergency vet clinic. She's muttering, "No, no, no …" Why hadn't she let go of Fred sooner?

Fred dies on the exam table. The ER vet offers an autopsy, but Jane declines. "Dead is dead," she manages to say. She wants to scream, pound her trembling fists, which stay obediently lined up on the metal table where Fred is, where he isn't anymore. She unfurls her fingers and lays a hand on his oh-so-elegant head. "Take as much time as you need," the vet says. Jane remembers saying that to the clients at her clinic. Vihaan pulls a chair to the exam table so she can sit while she keeps her hand on Fred. He is still warm. She doesn't want to wait until he feels even less alive.

Vihaan carries the empty carrier, while Jane signs a form opting not to come back for Fred's ashes.

At home, she closes herself in her bedroom to weep. After Amy died, Fred was such a consolation. With Fred gone, Amy is even more gone. At least Fred died at an age when Jane should have seen it coming. Now she chides herself. What a fool she's been to think that Amy still inhabited the world through Fred, as if Fred were a grandson who would outlive both Amy and Jane.

Amy stole opioids from Jane's clinic. Jane let her.

After Amy died, Jane's will to live came in part from being Fred's guardian and in part from being the keeper of Amy's existence. As time passed, she also wanted to read novels, wanted to eat strawberry rhubarb pie, and wanted to explore life with her co-op friends. She'd tricked herself into believing she was good at accepting that with every "before," there's an "after." What does being good at loss even mean?

She and Amy blackmailed each other.

She is most comfortable in the fetal position.

Barry makes her a smoothie and encourages her as she manages to choke it down. "Do you want to spend some time with Ginger Rogers?" he asks. Jane has always visited and cuddled Ginger daily. Until now. She doesn't know why she's reluctant, but the prospect of feeling Ginger's matted fur rumbling under her hand repels her.

"Someone should visit her," she says. "Will you?"

"I don't have your touch, but I'll try."

Jane keeps expecting to see Fred coming around the corner. She hears what sounds like Fred jumping onto the couch, but the thud is just Barry sitting down. She sees shadows and remembers that it's Fred's mealtime, except it isn't.

Amy had lived with the dealer.

She isn't hungry for anything except toast and tea. She can't afford to lose strength, but she does, and her tighter pants grow looser.

Amy returned home in exchange for Jane funding Amy's habit. They visited the dealer together. He had granite countertops. Jane thought about narcing on him but was worried about making the situation worse for Amy and for herself.

She uses sleep for grieving, as if waking hours were too few for the crushing, overtime job. In one phase of the night, she assigns herself Amy grief. She awakes from once again being unable to save Amy—Amy has no pulse. Jane tells herself that her next sleep task is to mourn Fred, and she dreams about him falling through her tremor-ridden hands, though he lands on his feet. Someone has left the front door open, and Fred tears away into the night. She knows she's lost him, but she keeps calling him nonetheless, her voice hoarse from the effort. She wakes up and says to the darkness, "Please."

Jane doled out the pills. Amy agreed to rehab, once, twice, three times.

She wishes for a memory eraser, though she wouldn't say such a thing to her housemates, who are all terrified of losing their memories. Just a day or two without grief, she reasons. Maybe that's what Amy sought in the drugs—a melting away of the past and the future. Barry has muscle relaxants. She could ask him for a few or steal them, but she doesn't know where he keeps them.

Jane kept the pills under lock and key.

She and Doris are on shopping duty this week. Think of the money you're saving on cat food, Jane tells herself with a grim smile as she follows Doris through the supermarket. The bulk of the items in the cart have been fetched by Doris, who is attending to the shopping list. Jane spends a long time comparing the price per ounce of different sizes and brands of raisins, then closes her eyes and takes the first box her hand touches. Living on the edge,

Jane thinks, and she smiles a real smile for the first time in days. She hitches up her loose pants.

At the dinner table, Jane nibbles a piece of toast as the others talk and laugh, a foreign language. All she can focus on is how she and her roommates are all old and will lose each other. Who will go first? Will it be sudden or slow?

"What are you thinking about, Jane?" asks Pearl, who has spinach between her two front teeth.

"I'm sorry. I'm just out of it." No point in voicing her morbid thoughts.

"That's okay," Ellen says.

Jane realizes she doesn't even know what day it is. She stands up, then sits down again. Pushing her plate out of the way, she lays her head on the table.

Barry pats her back. "Are you sick?" he asks.

"Just tired."

"I can help you get to bed," he says.

"It's not bedtime," she says into the table.

The group is quiet except for the percussion of silverware.

When she wakes up, she is alone, and the table has been cleared. Her leg is buzzing. When Amy was little, she cried when her arm fell asleep—her first pins and needles.

Amy threatened to kill herself if Jane didn't up the dosage.

It's time for the nightly grief shift, and her pink cotton nightgown with the sprigs of violets is her uniform. Sleep eludes her. Her mouth feels full of salt crystals, freeze-dried tears. Three a.m., then four a.m. As hard as she can, she slaps one of her tremulous hands with the other and feels satisfaction with the dose of pain. Experimentally, she bends back a finger until her eyes start watering.

Amy found the key to the medicine cabinet.

She'd thought she was choosing the best of lousy choices, and maybe she had prolonged Amy's life. If you'd peeked into their kitchen window, you'd have seen a mother stirring the sweet strawberry with the tart rhubarb while the daughter rolled out the dough.

The sun is starting to rise when Jane goes outside. She makes a clicking sound, and Ginger Rogers appears. The striped back, the white cheeks, so warm under Jane's fingers. In this moment, loving is worth the risk.

Chapter 4: Skating

Barry awakes to a headache and decides to distract himself from the cranial icepicks by browsing men online. Unfortunately, or fortunately, he isn't attracted to younger men these days, so the pickings are slimmer. After he reads a dozen profiles and takes a steaming shower, the pain in his head subsides.

It's his seventieth birthday, and he's been granted freedom from his chores for the day, his roommates filling in. English muffins, Dundee marmalade, and café au lait are his birthday breakfast requests, and all six of the roommates join in, the bright orange of the marmalade festive in and of itself.

Without the tether of household chores, Barry feels unmoored. The feeling reminds him of when he used to ice skate in Central Park and would change back into street shoes, the loosening of laces and the fullness of his whole foot navigating the friction-filled ground, strange until it became the norm again. Maybe he could go ice skating today. The temperature's supposed to be over 100 degrees this afternoon, and an icy rink appeals.

It's Sunday, so no one in the household is working. Doris, Pearl, Vihaan, and Jane want to come along to the skating rink, to flee the heat, and to drink hot chocolate. Now that Tomás and Ellen have reunited from their week of separation, they say they'll welcome having the house to themselves for a couple of hours.

"Nothing personal," Ellen says. Each of the co-opers admits to sometimes missing how it feels to have a place all to oneself.

Jane asks Barry, "Do you want us to skedaddle so you can have some time alone here?"

"Maybe some other day," Barry says.

"Should I invite Neighbor David to skate?" Doris asks.

"Sure."

Doris knocks on David's door, and he opens it, smiling. "To what do I owe this pleasure?" he asks. He uses the words he'd want her to say to him.

"Do you ice skate?" A curious warmth suffuses her chest.

"Used to as a kid."

Doris explains the planned afternoon outing, and David says, "I'm in." They shake hands. He might be thirty years younger than she, but he finds her appealing—elegant in her crisp white blouse with her auburn hair and silver hoop earrings. He wonders whose idea it was to invite him to skate.

He dons long pants for the first time in months. When he gets in the Odyssey with the neighbors, he says to Barry, "Congratulations. You made it."

Pearl bends over Barry's rental skates, tightening the laces. She pats his knee and straightens his watch cap. He's dressed in his old uniform of black jeans, hundred-dollar cotton black tee, and supple, flattering black leather jacket. Lady Gaga's "Bad Romance" provides the background music as he enters the rink, one tentative footstep after another. Gaga is singing, "I don't want to be friends." His ankles wobble. Two men in hockey skates and jerseys whiz by. It's okay to be slow, he tells himself. With a pang, he recalls his younger self and how busy he'd kept back in New

York. With his swift stride, he'd weave between other sidewalk pedestrians as if on an obstacle course. He'd gulped his days rather than sipped.

Now he's gliding, remembering to keep his knees bent for stability. He doesn't recognize the next songs coming over the loudspeakers, but they're catchy enough for him to sway back and forth as he goes. He notices a girl who couldn't be more than three years old shakily walking on the ice, plopping down, springing up, falling down again, so short the distance for her between standing upright and sitting on the ice. She doesn't know yet to be upset about falling.

Doris is ahead in her red-and-black plaid jacket. She pumps her legs, rides the momentum, pumps again. The muscle memory fills her with security and cheer at how something she could do a long time ago comes back.

David is less sure of himself, pushing off from the wall, smooth sailing leading to doubts and back to gripping the wall. It's hard for him to distinguish between caution and unnecessary constraint.

In the middle of the rink are the most skilled figure skaters. One is like a top, spinning so fast that Barry sees her as a blur. He skates another lap, then another. He pictures his leg bones as matte silver like the blades on the skates, the warmth covering the bones a maple syrup. He smiles at how his life still revolves around food.

An older man enters the rink, and he looks a bit like one of the more eligible prospects from Barry's earlier online browsing. The man is short, as is Barry, and slim, as Barry is not. He has a lot more hair than Barry and wears red glasses. With his hands clasped behind his back, the man seems to float over the ice.

"Eyes on the road," says Doris as she catches up to Barry. She takes his hand, and he squeezes hers.

He says, "We're doing this. We can still do it."

"Indeed."

David watches Barry and Doris circling the rink hand in hand. He thinks of shaking Doris's hand earlier, her prominent veins and knuckles, a translucent hand with character, history. His hands are cold, and he shoves them in his pockets.

"How does it feel?" Jane asks Barry when he joins the group at one of the tables overlooking the rink.

"Not as easy as it used to, but marvelous. A privilege."

Pearl treats Barry to hot chocolate with whipped cream. He struggles to be patient with the drink's heat, not wanting to burn his tongue.

The man with the red glasses sits on a nearby bench to tighten his skate laces. Unlike the well-worn rental skates, this man's skates are polished and more supportive looking, the sturdy skates of someone who visits the rink frequently. The man catches Barry's eye and nods. Barry raises his paper cup to the man. They smile.

Vihaan asks, "Do you know him?"

"No," Barry says and laughs.

"You're such a Greg," Pearl calls Barry, aka "Gregarious."

Feeling steadier on the ice, David catches up to Doris, and he wishes he could offer her his hand. His physical contact with other people is limited to their overtures—the platonic hug he gets from his ex when they hang out at his house and watch movies, the "good game" handshake Vihaan gives him when they play their weekly tennis match.

"Clear the ice," the loudspeakers announce.

It's time for the Zamboni to resurface the ice, smoothing down the gouges, melting the buildup of what looks like snow.

"I need to be Zamboni-ed," says Pearl.

"You're radiating cold," Jane says to David. "It's refreshing." Still, with concerted effort, she tries to button the top button of her cardigan. Pearl wants to help but knows that Jane is proud about such things.

Vihaan sees how closely David and Doris are sitting together. He also notices how the man with the red glasses is standing quite near their table. Vihaan catches Barry's eye and points with his chin toward to the other man. Barry raises an eyebrow.

The anniversary of Vihaan's wife's death is approaching. He doubts he would have rejoined the co-op if she'd survived the cancer. In a parallel life, he and his wife stroll the neighborhood where they'd lived in Tucson, nodding to neighbors, discussing what to have for dinner. They'd moved to Tucson for her graduate school, so long ago, and stayed. He doesn't believe in any kind of afterlife but knows his wife would be pleased to see him surrounded by friends. She'd worried that he was too dependent on her, which he probably was, though he hadn't wanted to admit it to her, or to himself.

The rink is glossy again. Barry, Doris, and David return to the ice after the younger people and the man with the red glasses resume the counterclockwise flow.

"I have a few more laps in me," Barry says. He's already imagining skating more often, maybe running into the man with the red glasses. His ankles would grow stronger, his balance improve.

Doris says, "I'm going to go for a fast one, relatively speaking." And she's off. As when she folk dances, she experiences the music as a benign odorless smoke ribboning the air, cushioning her legs and arms, helping her defy gravity, a smoke so different from a wildfire smoke.

The hockey skaters zip by, startling her so that she almost trips but rights herself just in time. She's annoyed by and envious of their speed. The men are like daredevil motorcyclists surprising the slower vehicles, appearing out of nowhere and zooming past. Damn them.

A woman up ahead falls backward, her head hitting the ice with a sickening thud. Another skater, unable to swerve in time, runs over the woman's outstretched hand. Doris winces, and her heart races.

The rink's safety guard blows a whistle. "Out of the way, folks," he shouts. The crowd around the fallen woman parts.

David and Barry are at Doris's side, asking what happened. They lean against the wall.

"She really hit her head. I hope she's all right."

The woman struggles to sit up with the safety guard's assistance. Her hand is bleeding, pooling on the ice next to her, bloodying her white sweater. Leaning against the safety guard, the woman stands up. They make their shaky way off the ice where staff members are waiting to help her, ushering her into a back room behind the rental counter.

Doris makes herself inhale to the count of five, hold it, and exhale slowly.

"Are you okay?" David asks her.

"Just catching my breath."

In the waiting area, the roommates are leaning against the plexiglass that tops the half-wall around the rink. A concerned cheering section, they wave at their friends on the ice. "The friends are watching," David says. He waves back, and Doris and Barry do too.

Shaken, Barry thinks how any one of them could have fallen, fallen hard. The woman who fell might have a concussion. Shouldn't the staff members have cleared the ice? Put orange cones around the blood at least? The relentless circling of the other skaters seems both callous and resilient.

"That's why the rink had us sign the waivers," Doris says, as if reading Barry's mind.

The safety guard is back, mopping up the blood, the evidence. Barry skates up to him and asks, "Is she all right?"

"Her friend is going to drive her to a clinic."

"That's good."

Barry, David, and Doris huddle again and agree to take a break. Back at the friends' table, they debate whether it's too big a risk to keep skating. Pearl and Jane are worried. Vihaan says, "Everything's a gamble." He feels like a hypocrite. He'd passed on the skating because he was loath to endanger his tennis fitness.

Barry entertains the risk of saying hello to the man with the red glasses. "A gamble," he says aloud.

Pearl has been thinking of whether to leave her underpaid library job. Not worth the risk of no income. She also wants to avoid having more free time because she wouldn't know what to do with it.

Jane considers the continued risk of attaching herself to the roommates. Not just roommates, they are teammates.

Doris imagines the risk of asking David if he'd like to go folk dancing with her.

David sighs. It's safer just to forget the flicker he feels around Doris. Forgetting would be the mature thing to do, or maybe just enjoying the spark without wanting it to grow.

Jane shivers and asks if anyone wants to warm up on a bench outside with her. Nodding, Pearl says yes and puts her arm around Jane.

Barry says, "Why don't we call it an afternoon soon? But first, I have to do something."

He's not ready just yet for street shoes. Back on the ice, he follows the man with the red glasses, who's too fast for Barry to catch up with and maybe it's just as well. Surely this is a different man than the fellow online—a straight man or a taken man. Even if it is the man online, it's a long road between meeting someone's surface and finding his depth.

Seventy years old, full of longing as far back as he can remember. First it was literal hunger, food so scarce in his family. In his early teens, he'd longed to be straight. Later, he'd longed for a family of friends. He'd longed for coworkers who were friends too. He wonders if he still needs more than he already has. His right blade catches in an ice gouge. He lurches forward, his knee touches the ice, but he pulls himself up. Just one more lap.

The man with the red glasses is at his side. "Are you enjoying this?" he asks.

"Absolutely. A bit shaky. You seem to be at home on the ice."

"I'm here for an hour most afternoons around this time."

"I'd like to come back soon, build my sea legs."

The man has a gracious smile, the kind Barry had when he'd welcomed customers to his restaurant. They exchange names. The man is Cliff, which makes Barry think of the ice-skating challenge: not to fall, as in fall off a cliff.

"I imagine I'll see you here again," says Barry.

"Please feel free to say hello. I'm usually in my own world but welcome a friendly face," Cliff says. He floats off.

Barry rejoins Doris and David, who have returned their skates. Doris is rubbing her hands together and talking with David about her folk dancing group. Barry dons his street shoes. No more gliding today.

Barry tells his friends he's going to take a nap. First, he lies in bed and searches for the listing of the man who looks like Cliff. No, this is another man. Barry vacillates between disappointment and relief—disappointment that it won't be easy to shoot off an email to Cliff and relief that it won't be that easy to contact him. He can wait to go back to the rink, or he can never go. He rubs his feet, which are still tense from skating.

The housemates working on dinner makes for pleasant background music. Again, they'd asked before the last supermarket run what he'd like for a birthday dinner, and as at breakfast, he wants to keep it simple but indulgent, a day not to worry about preventing a heart attack. He'd requested a cheese-and-fruit plate, hearty bread with a thick crust, and red wine.

A couple of birthdays ago, he'd still owned the restaurant, though he was spending less and less time there, letting go of his usual control, allowing the younger employees to step up. The restaurant had come of age and didn't need his supervision, a bittersweet stage of ownership.

Ellen arranges the fruit on the platter, a palette of peaches, plums, mango, and kiwi, while Tomás unwraps hard and soft cheeses. They place a dish of Marcona almonds and one of kalamata olives on the table.

When they were alone in the house earlier that day, they tried making love for the first time in what seemed like ages. After they'd given up and taken a nap, they awoke to more responsive bodies. "That was a surprise," Ellen said as she laid her head on Tomás's chest and he kissed her hair. She's self-conscious about her hair thinning but had willed herself to let go and accept the love. Now, as Tomás slices the bread, she admires his elegant fingers.

With a soft cloth, Pearl polishes the wine glasses. She removes her eyeglasses and wipes away the smudges on them too. For this occasion, the group has sprung for a more expensive couple of bottles, and Pearl is looking forward to seeing if she can tell the difference.

Jane has had trouble warming up since the rink, so she sits outside in the sauna-like heat, scratching Ginger behind the ears. A ladder-backed woodpecker with its red cap taps away in the crepe myrtle, but the cat doesn't seem to notice.

Vihaan consults Doris. "We can't do this without a cake," he says.

"Let's sneak out to the bakery," Doris says. There they browse the options, settling on chocolate with a mirror glaze and fondant roses. They are both aware that seldom do they purchase any food besides the groceries. A $5 hot chocolate and a $30 cake seem frivolous, but if not for Barry's birthday, when will they have another excuse?

On the drive home, Vihaan says, "What do you think of Neighbor David?"

"Do you think he's an old soul? You know him from tennis."

"I think he's a gentle soul. Earnest."

"Nothing wrong with that." She's perspiring, her hands damp on the cake box. She thinks of older women with younger men in *The Graduate* and *The Last Picture Show* and how the movies portray the older women as pathetic.

They gather around the dining table, an Ella Fitzgerald and Louis Armstrong record playing in the background.

"Barry was flirting with a man at the skating rink," Pearl announces to Ellen and Tomás.

"What's this?" Tomás asks.

"That wasn't the only drama," Barry says. "A woman fell and hit her head." He spreads cheese on a slice of bread and takes a sizable bite.

"That's scary," Ellen says. "Glad you and Doris are safe and sound." Tomás passes her the platter. The closeness in bed with him makes her feel like restricting her food again, searching for a sense of control, an exhausting mirage that captivated her for so many years. Cheese equals protein, fat, and calcium, she tells herself, which will lubricate her mind and build her bones. She extends the platter to Jane, whose hands are too shaky to grip it, and she also serves herself.

Vihaan says, "Tell us what the man is like, Barry. I saw you talking on the ice."

"He's a rink regular. Cliff. Good taste in eyewear and an engaging smile," Barry says. "I may go back to the rink sometime soon." Why the hell not.

Maybe it's the placebo effect, but Pearl is finding the wine particularly tasty as she swirls it in her mouth. She nods yes.

Soon the platter is empty save for a few cheese rinds, and the friends lean back in their chairs.

"I'll get tea water started," Doris says. "Vihaan, want to give me a hand?"

In the kitchen, Vihaan lights seven candles. He carries out the cake, Doris the plates and forks. They come out singing, and the others join in a motley chorus. The gloss on the cake reminds Barry of the ice in the skating rink smoothed by the Zamboni.

"Cuppa Earl Grey with a spot of moo, Barry?"

"Splendid. Thank you." He has learned to voice positive thoughts when he has them. "I can't think of anywhere I'd rather be than at our table with you folks, eating chocolate cake."

For those of the group who haven't already had kindred thoughts this evening, they do now.

"We love you," Jane says, a stretch for her.

Barry is in bed, but in his mind's eye, he's at the rink. He wears a pair of skates that are more supportive than those he wore today, and the blades are sharp and gleaming. He is about to catch up with Cliff when one of the hockey skaters rams him from behind. When he overcompensates by leaning backward, he falls, his head hitting the ice. The hockey skater yanks Barry upright, and he sees that the skater is his old boyfriend, the one with the husband, who, as the kids say, ghosted him. For some reason, the pain in his head evaporates, and he shoves the hockey skater away. The benign detachment with which he'd come to view his ex has receded. The safety guard escorts the hockey skater from the rink, and Barry breathes in chilly air, breathes in peace.

Does he want the drama of meeting someone new?

He's perspiring and thirsty, so he gets out of bed and heads to the kitchen for a glass of water. Jane is at the table. He sits next to her and leans his head on her shoulder. She runs a hand over his head the way she does with her feline friends.

"Sometimes I'm scared," Barry whispers.

He's unsure whether she heard him because she doesn't respond right away. Then she whispers back, "I am too."

Chapter 5: Maintenance

Pearl first notices the woman's unwashed smell, which makes Pearl hold her breath around her. After she leaves her library job each day, the smell lingers in her nostrils and on her clothes. At home, she asks her roommates if they can smell anything, and they say no. Still, feeling somewhat ashamed of her disgust, she gargles with Listerine and changes her clothes each evening.

The library hosts homeless people more often during the sweltering or the frigid weather, when everyone seeks air conditioning or heat. This is a summer with a record number of hundred-degree-plus days, and it's not even August yet. Back in Flint, more people would have died in the heat. While Austin residents suffer, they've worked up to the boil slowly.

It's hard to tell how old the woman is, but she's probably as old as Pearl. Grime has settled in her wrinkles, and her hair is a tangle the color of curdled milk. She has a tight-lipped smile, as if she's afraid of exposing her teeth. When Pearl was young, she'd had an awful overbite and used to hide her teeth too.

Pearl runs into the woman in the bathroom, where the woman is attempting a paper towel bath. "How are you?" Pearl asks.

"I could complain, but I won't." With arthritic fingers, she tries to comb her hair, gets her fingers stuck, and ends up just patting it into submission. "You work with the kids, eh? I've seen you." She is missing a few teeth.

"Yes. I'm Pearl."

"That's funny. I'm Ruby. I was a kid once."

Pearl fetches a couple of chocolate chip cookies from the break room, wraps them in a napkin, and leaves the package on top of one of the bags that Ruby has parked next to a chair near the periodicals. A copy of AARP magazine is on the chair seat.

Ruby returns to her chair, picks up the package, opens it, and sniffs. She looks around, and Pearl shifts her gaze to the returns that she's sorting.

Pearl walks the six blocks home, pausing to admire a beautyberry bush and the esperanzas that must have been a dozen feet tall. Before Barry suggested that the co-opers reunite, Pearl had been doing the math, trying to figure out how long she could live on her diminished Social Security and low paycheck. She'd either have to work into her mid-90s or become homeless or kick the bucket as soon as she stopped working. If she became ill, she would have crumbled under hefty medical bills. And what would she do when Social Security and Medicare, as projected, trickled away? It was an unsolvable puzzle that she'd tried to ignore.

She thinks she sees Ruby up ahead, veering into the thicket that lines the park. When she's strolled through the park, she's heard kids talking about the bogeymen who live there.

Ruby joins the kids for story time one afternoon. She slumps on a chair in the back, and some of the children turn around and stare. They whisper to their parents. Pearl manages to entrance the children again by hamming it up, conjuring hokey voices for the various characters.

After story time, Pearl notices Ruby at the water fountain, gulping for what seems like minutes. She remembers Flint and its contaminated water. Ruby passes Pearl and says, "Hydration. Very important."

"That's what they say."

"The influential 'they.'"

Back at home, Pearl struggles to resist her cleanup routine, to distract herself from the lingering smell. She does her nodding meditation, chin up and down, but she gives in to the cleanup process after half an hour of trying to suppress the urge. She'd once had a dog that had developed a tumor in his throat, and as the cancer progressed, the dog smelled like rot. She remembers cuddling and falling asleep with the dog on the nights before the only merciful path was to say goodbye. Love had outweighed her senses.

After work another day, Ruby leaves the library at the same time Pearl does. It doesn't grow cooler in the evenings, so the effect of stepping outside is like having warm soup thrown in your face. Ruby is heading in Pearl's direction, and they share the sidewalk side by side. As they pass an apartment complex, Ruby says, "I used to live there."

Pearl doesn't want to pry about what happened, but Ruby offers it up. "I lost my job at Walmart because no matter when I left the house, the buses were late, and I was supposed to catch two of them. I couldn't afford the rent or electricity anymore."

They are passing the ice cream shop with the purple and green life-size cows on the patio. "Could I treat you to an ice cream cone?" Pearl asks. She is still hungry from the dinner of cottage cheese and fruit that she wolfed down in the break room an hour ago.

"Oh, you don't need to do that."

"But I'd like to."

At the counter, the other customers fan out to be farther away from Ruby and Pearl. Ruby studies the shop's bulletin board while Pearl pays for the cones.

At their table, Ruby arranges her bags around her as if they were bodyguards. She says, "Well, I told you something about me. What about you?"

Pearl ends up talking about what Austin was like back in her college days. Ruby went to the university too and majored in philosophy. An hour passes quickly. Pearl polishes off her cone long before Ruby, who is clearly savoring hers.

They part ways near the park.

Pearl is so busy telling the housemates about Ruby that she delays her cleanup routine until Jane wrinkles her nose and tells her that she can indeed smell something.

At breakfast the next morning, Pearl asks her housemates, "What would you feel if I invited Ruby over for a shower and laundry?"

The housemates are silent except for the clink of Vihaan's spoon in his oatmeal bowl.

Pearl offers, "I'd clean up afterward."

More silence.

"Somebody?"

"I'm uncomfortable with it," Doris says, her tone tight. Doris, Pearl's closest friend in the house, betraying her.

"I don't know," Barry says.

"I feel wary," says Ellen. She takes a long sip of her tea.

"I'm with Ellen," Tomás says.

Of course you are, Pearl thinks. She clenches her hands, sets her jaw. She is nodding to herself, feeling her eye twitch.

"How bad could it be?" Vihaan asks.

"Did you smell Pearl yesterday?" Jane asks.

"Sorry, Perla," Tomás says.

She stands up and clears her plate. They're all so selfish. She wishes she lived alone, no decisions by committee. She holes up in her room, pacing back and forth, and she doesn't say goodbye when she leaves for work the next day. At the end of the cul-de-sac, she crouches down near the feral cat group, and the cats eye her, keep their distance. Squirrels in the trees make teasing chirrups at the cats.

Maybe she's being presumptuous by assuming Ruby wants what she would want—to be clean. And maybe it would be a slippery slope to invite over Ruby. Being clean doesn't last, just as being full doesn't, just as being well rested doesn't. So much of life is maintenance.

Ruby is dozing, snoring softly, in what has become her chair, vinyl that gets wiped off with disinfectant spray by the night cleaning staff. The only other sounds besides Ruby's snoring are kids and their parents whispering and the faint clack of patrons typing on computers. Libraries have always felt like houses of worship to Pearl. Pearl's fantasy as a kid was to hide out as the library closed and spend the night wandering the aisles, dipping into books for all ages, curling up on a chair where hundreds of other patrons have sat and escaped to other worlds.

Pearl is quiet at dinner, and the conversation swirls around her. She is remembering when she left Ann Arbor to work at the public library in Flint. Her parents didn't understand why she'd take a job with "those people." Though they'd visited her in Ann Arbor, they never visited her in Flint. When her first lease was up, she moved to a smaller apartment, giving up on her family enjoying the guest room, donating the guest bed and the extra pillows her parents could have enjoyed. Her sister resented her for not moving back home to help with their parents when later they needed extra care. Pearl took the guilt trip as far as relieving her sister whenever she had vacation and contributing to the hefty nursing fees. She chides herself for how freshly piercing the splinter with her parents can be if she lets it be. It's ridiculous. They've been gone for more than twenty years.

The next night, the roommates announce that they've changed their minds about Ruby coming over.

"She could be any one of us," Ellen says.

"It seems like the humane thing to do," Jane says. "Not everything has to smell good."

Vihaan says, "It's always good to help someone."

For a moment, Pearl is nodding but unsettled. Now she'll have to follow up, have to think of a way not to shame Ruby with the invitation. After work later that week, she asks Ruby if she'd like to get ice cream. Ruby is delicately working on her cone when Pearl blurts out, "Do you have a place to take a shower?"

Ruby seems to ponder her answer and ends up saying, "I get by."

"Would you like to come over sometime and use our shower?"

Ruby looks suspicious. "Who's 'our'?"

"I have housemates. They're harmless."

Ruby wants to hear about them, so Pearl gives thumbnail bios of the other co-opers.

"You're lucky," Ruby says.

"So much is luck."

"When would be a good time for me to take a shower?"

Pearl arranges to walk with Ruby to West House on a Saturday afternoon. The sun is still blasting, and both women have sweat circles under their arms and around the necklines of their shirts. Pearl holds her shirt away from her body to get ventilation. The beautyberries shine purple. Pearl notices that she's shuffling instead of picking up her feet. When did that happen?

Apparently having seen Pearl and Ruby approaching the house, Barry opens the front door. "Welcome," he says. He introduces himself and extends his hand.

Ruby's shoulders are up by her ears, and she seems both shy and eager while meeting the house members who aren't out shopping or melting on the tennis court.

Ruby unearths a load of laundry from her plastic bags, and Pearl lends her a pair of elastic-waisted shorts and an oversize tee so they can launder Ruby's current outfit. She gives Ruby a travel-size deodorant that she'd bought in the vague hope of traveling, but she doesn't have the means or a destination.

The roommates are walking by more often than seems normal. Several murmur in the living room.

While Ruby is in the shower, Pearl puts the laundry on the highest temperature and longest cycle. Barry had installed a water heater with endless hot water, handy for such a large household. Pearl washes her hands for a long time.

Ruby emerges from the bathroom with the towel wrapped turban style around her head. Despite her outfit, which she's donned with her duct-taped sneakers, she looks almost regal. Her skin has lost the grime and looks more fragile than usual. "Do you have something for me to clean the shower?" she asks, and Pearl provides her with an all-purpose lemon-scented cleaning spray and a fresh sponge.

Pearl feels pressure to help the time pass quickly while Ruby's laundry is finishing. When in doubt, make cookies, she concludes. Ruby sips iced tea—"Hydration!"—and keeps her company on a kitchen stool while Pearl bustles around the kitchen assembling and mixing the ingredients listed on the back of the Quaker oatmeal box.

"Cookies," Pearl calls when the first batch comes out.

Housemates gather. Vihaan's back from his game, and the sweat pours out of him. The conversation is amiable but limited to subjects like favorite cookies and the weather. Pearl breathes in and can only smell the cinnamon and vanilla.

After Ruby leaves with a fresher, sturdier set of plastic bags, Doris says, "That wasn't bad. I'm sorry I was a scaredy-cat."

Pearl hugs her. "Thanks for being gracious."

"I wonder where she's off to now," Barry says.

***

Ruby's visits become a weekly routine. Once when she's at the co-op later in the day, her laundry in the dryer, she asks if she can make cheese omelets for the group. She'd been a cook at a diner when she was younger. After dinner, they play Apples to Apples with Ruby's pairings often being the cleverest. She and Barry shared a philosophy professor in college, and the two of them click. They sit in the living room, hydrating, and Ruby asks numerous questions about Barry's restaurant, to which he gives lengthy answers and shows her reviews.

Ruby's absent from the library. At first, Pearl keeps looking over at her chair, but other patrons come and go from it.

Ruby misses the day she usually comes over to West House. A knock at the door perks up Pearl, but it's Neighbor David meeting with Doris for a walk.

Pearl starts taking walks in the park where she'd seen Ruby heading when they went their separate ways. She peers into the thicket and spots sleeping bags but no people. At the green edge of the duck pond with its algae looking like grass, Pearl stands and stares. A toddler steps into the muck and slides under the water until the father rushes in for a rescue.

The weeks go by, and the roommates speculate about what could have happened to Ruby. She's in a hospital. She got arrested for camping in the city. Or worse. Pearl doesn't even know Ruby's last name. She starts googling "Austin" plus "homeless" plus "dead," and she braces as she reads the tragic news stories, but none of them are about Ruby.

The housemates stop talking about her.

Pearl attends a workshop for the children's librarians at the central library downtown, a few miles from her library. As she leaves the conference room to take a bathroom break, she passes a row of chairs tucked into the stacks.

Ruby is asleep in one of the chairs. She has on the oversize tee that Pearl had ended up giving her. Pearl freezes, unsure of what to do. Her eyes fill, both with relief and irritation.

Ruby opens an eye and registers Pearl. Pearl waves, Ruby waves back, then closes her eyes again. Pearl continues standing there until it's clear that Ruby has either fallen asleep again or is pretending to have. At least she's safe, though her arms look thinner and have a few purple bruises.

She wants to ask Ruby why she didn't say goodbye, but she knows Ruby has her reasons. She is not Pearl.

Back at home, Pearl reports the news to the roommates.

"Why didn't you talk to her?" Jane asks.

Pearl nods. Her answer, "She knows where to find me," just begets other questions from the roommates and questions of her own. She hazards guesses, but this is a test for which she's unprepared.

She thinks she smells Ruby on her sleeve but knows it's her imagination. She'd saved the sponge that Ruby used to clean the shower after she bathed. It's important to toss it right away now.

Chapter 6: Patience

Vihaan lies on the couch, his knee throbbing as if it's straining to burst through his skin and be free. When teaching a student on the court, he twisted the knee, yelped in pain, and had to go to a clinic, where he was told that nothing major had gone awry. He's supposed to use that leg as little as possible.

Back in the day, an ankle injury had ruined his tournament career, and he'd gone through countless sessions of physical therapy, acupuncture, and bereavement counseling the year after it had happened. He never played another tournament.

He feels like he's going through withdrawal symptoms. He's shaky, cross, craving movement, and he's pissed off at people who can walk normally and people who somehow can sit still. He tests the knee by walking down the cul-de-sac with Barry, but he has to lean on Barry to get back to the house. From overcompensating, his other leg hurts.

He monopolizes the couch, setting up shop there for the day with a spill-proof cup of ice water, a bag of turkey jerky that Doris bought him as a consolation prize, a boring history of Arizona that induces sleep, and a more captivating biography of Arthur Ashe that Pearl brought home from the library. He misses Jane's cat Fred who would sometimes share the couch with him when Jane was occupied in the kitchen.

He'd read somewhere that bed-ridden pianists are better able to resume playing if they visualize themselves doing so during their convalescence. Vihaan sees himself with just-the-right grip on the racket, doing an overhead serve, grunting, the thwack of the ball. Here comes the ball, and he returns it, again and again. He wins, of course, against his shadowy opponent.

The sun pours in through the windows, sometimes making him squeeze his eyes shut. He is thirsty for this natural light, which he needs to ward off the blues. The hours pass slowly except when he has a companion. Doris volunteers to massage his good leg, and he finds this soothing, even erotic, and he hopes she doesn't notice the latter. He finds himself having pangs of jealousy about her friendship with Neighbor David, but he wonders why a greater interest in her has awakened now that she's hanging out with David more. He knows he takes for granted what he has, perhaps an opportunity to woo her, until it starts receding or, in the use of his protesting knee, screeches to a halt.

Someday, if he lives long enough, he'll be unable to move the way he, for the most part, moves now. Someday, in all likelihood, he will experience pain for longer than he ever has. He might reach ten on a pain scale of one to ten. Maybe he could use this time—the present—to build his tolerance for what his teeming brain insists is intolerable. These ponderings lead to a surge of fire in his knee. Cool water, he reassures himself, and he calls out to Ellen, who's in the kitchen, to fetch him, please, an icepack from the freezer.

"Are you bored?" Ellen asks.

"I'm feeling sorry for myself."

"Would you like me to feel sorry for you too?"

"Please. Also, I'm spending too much time with the news."

"That'll keep you down."

He considers putting his phone, the source of his news, in timeout, but there's the instant masochistic gratification of being more informed about the woes of the world.

Barry has set up a shower chair, and Vihaan looks forward to the time each day when he can sit there and allow the warm water to rain on him. He remembers his wife, Rose, and how, during a rare rain, they sometimes donned their swimsuits and sat in the backyard, getting soaked. His usual shower technique had been in and out, waste no water, but now somehow, the minutes fly by until he forces himself to stand up and hop out, careful not to slip.

That night he wakes with an urgency to use the bathroom. He risks using his bad knee to get there quickly, and he pays for it the next day as the knee seems to be using a screechy voice to scold him. Somehow the knee has taken on a persona, is separate but has chained the rest of his body to it. He worries that he's undone whatever had been knitting together for the good.

"Is there something special between you and David?" Vihaan asks Doris one afternoon. The weather is gloomy, too dark for this time of day, and he feels deflated enough to risk asking her for what he's concerned will be bad news for him.

"We're friends. If I'd given birth when I was fifteen, and my son or daughter had a child, David, when he or she was fifteen, I could be his grandmother."

"That's an interesting way to calculate it."

He hopes she'll ask why he was inquiring, though she doesn't. He doesn't know what he'd say anyway. He has to live in the same house with her, whether or not she's interested in deepening their affection, and it might be awkward to reveal anything. On the other hand, Barry's seeming lack of concern for what might be uncomfortable is inspiring, and Vihaan can detect that influence on his thoughts, if not his actions.

Resentment at Rose dying before he did bubbles up, a metallic taste in his mouth. He'd been considering lunch but loses his appetite.

Doris had lost her spouse too, but she'd had decades before that of being single and presumably knew the ins and outs of that state better than Vihaan did. Being single seemed a skill that was hard to learn at his age. Before Rose died, she named single friends of hers who might be interested in him. "I could talk to Nancy or Jacqueline," she said, to which he gave her a vehement, "No way." Nancy and Jacqueline visited, and he tried to read whether they were eyeing him in an assessing way, as if he were a used vehicle that could use a lemon inspection before they committed. He was deliberately reserved with them, and after Rose died, he hid in a different aisle of the supermarket if he spotted them in produce.

He can smell his own perspiration and wonders if he forgot to apply deodorant. All the sweating he did when playing tennis, and especially afterward, had been cathartic, as if he were purging toxins. Now those toxins are trapped in him, chewing his innards. If he could cry, that might help, but his crying ability is like a tool rusty from disuse, and perhaps his tears would come out gritty and orange.

He has a pain in the calf of his injured leg. Great—a blood clot. He chews too many baby aspirin, and that seems to help, even if it may be the placebo effect.

Tomás finds Vihaan a captive audience, and he insists on teaching him how to make an origami crane. At first, Vihaan is frustrated and doesn't see how he can muster the fine motor skills required, but Tomás persists. By the end of the week, Vihaan has learned enough to pile up a dozen cranes on the coffee table, even if they look a bit like ugly ducklings.

Doris asks about Vihaan's son and suggests he call him. Vihaan has been talking himself out of doing so for a long time, the last time they spoke having been on the son's birthday six months ago. Do it for Rose, he thinks. He fears the awkwardness, not having anything to offer up about himself, and he decides to put it off.

Doris talks about her deceased parents' dementia, how their bodies stubbornly persisted after their brains shut down. "My mother didn't speak anymore. For months. Then I was playing Cole Porter's 'Let's Do It,' and I hear her whisper, 'Even educated fleas do it.'" Doris laughs, then gulps in air as if water has gone down the wrong way, and her eyes fill.

Vihaan reaches out and takes her hand, and they sit that way in silence until they hear nearby footsteps and drop hands.

Barry pokes his head in the living room, gives them a toothy grin, then does an about-face.

That night Vihaan hums "Let's Do It" to lull himself to sleep. With a start, he remembers all the money he's losing by having to take a break from coaching, and this makes sleep fitful. He can't get his knee to shut up. He envisions that fateful twist on the court when he'd been playing with such abandon. That was his mistake.

Neighbor David comes by with a knee-walker that he's borrowed from a friend who had knee replacement surgery. It's a scooter of sorts with which you use your good leg to propel you forward and rest your bum leg on a platform. Vihaan hops outside and tries it, doing figure eights on the smooth part of the street where the sinkhole was fixed. He returns inside with it and navigates too fast down the hall and slams into the kitchen counter. "Not hurt," he calls out. He wonders why the clinic didn't suggest this device instead of the wooden crutches they gave him that are unused because they hurt his armpits.

He, Doris, and David take a walk, and he sails down the sidewalks, the breeze ruffling his hair. David jogs next to him to be his spotter, and as they wait for Doris to catch up, Vihaan says,

"You and Doris have been hanging out more. Something special?"

David looks at Vihaan with wide eyes and sputters, "Just friends." He takes off his glasses and wipes them with his shirt.

"You keeping in shape without our tennis games?"

"I went to the court to see if I could practice my serve, and there was a woman there doing the same thing. We batted the ball around, and we're going to meet up again."

"That's great!" Vihaan says, detecting the strain in his voice. This has been the month of jealousy, a feeling he only remembers from when he witnessed over and over again how well his wife and son got along, their easy patter, so much more natural than his with his son. He and his son stopped talking about Rose not long after she died. Maybe his son doesn't feel free to talk about her. Maybe in their next conversation he could ask his son whether he's been thinking about his mother, and Vihaan could volunteer how much he misses her—her unflagging optimism, the way she remembered details about people she loved that they didn't even remember themselves, her ability to give undivided attention with that gaze, those velvet eyes the color of espresso. Surely, he and his son could turn Rose's absence into a bond instead of letting themselves drift further apart, letting the silence overcome them.

Doris catches up, and they do a U-turn to get back home.

He calls his son, Will, half-hoping it will go to voicemail. He'd forgotten how deep Will's voice is. When Vihaan brings up Rose, Will is wordless for a long time, and there's a sound as if he's blowing his nose. Will says, "I thought you were forgetting her. Forgetting me."

"Maybe I was avoiding. I'm so sorry." Vihaan's rusty tears leak out. "Will you let me try harder?"

"It's just going to be awkward between us," Will says. "Isn't it?"

"There are worse things," Vihaan says.

"Much worse things," Will agrees. "I think Mom was hoping we'd fill the gap."

Vihaan's knee grows stronger and quieter. He's too afraid to look at the calendar to see how long it's been, the weeks having blended together in boredom, in anticipation and enjoyment of time shared with Doris, and in 3 p.m. showers. Every time he's finished a bag of turkey jerky, a new one appears in the morning, thanks to Doris and the group.

He's well enough to be back on the chore rotation, and he tries to make up for lost time by taking on the task of another roommate each day. He also makes fifty samosas so the group will have substantial leftovers after they devour a mess of them with mint and mango chutneys.

He's now able to do physical therapy without the threat of further injury. Doris, who finally got a Texas license, drives him to the sessions and sits in the waiting area reading while he tries to be a patient patient.

He's back on the court with David, though taking it easy. He matches up the students who are at approximately the same level and does most of his coaching from the sidelines. He's perspiring enough to feel cleansed, and one day he licks the back of his hand for the salt taste.

It's hard to learn to trust himself again as he runs and pivots. At one moment, he pictures injuring himself again so he can return to the couch and Doris's soothing company. He misses her, but she's inside him now, and he can hear what she hasn't said outright: you're still here, and so am I.

Chapter 7: The Flow

INSTEAD OF FLEEING the wildfire, Doris is sitting in her old San Diego house. She's pulled a chair to the open front window and squints to best focus on the houses across the street, fascinating in their coats of pink and orange flames, sunset colors. Clouds of smoke shape-shift to float into her living room, as she's invited them, and she tries to gulp the smoke, tasting the chemical residue of what has burned.

Now she's awake, thankfully in Austin, her sleep mask soaked with perspiration, her relief acting as a fan to cool her. Still, she prowls the quiet house, sniffing for something burning, her hands twitching involuntarily as Jane's do. She's a dazed animal trying to shake off a blow. Moonlight pours through the living room windows, and the tiny red and green lights of appliances and electronic devices also interrupt the unwelcome darkness. She hears Barry snoring, and while normally she finds the sound grating, it soothes her.

Fear makes her hungry, so she downs two bowls of Cheerios on which she's shaken generous amounts of brown sugar. She drinks two glasses of chilled water. Now she can go back to sleep, her full belly a protective padding. Sleep, the rescuer and the abyss.

Vihaan is still in recovery from a knee injury, and Doris wants to spend more time with him, to comfort him. She spends money on organic turkey jerky as a treat for him, figuring she'll scrimp on buying treats for herself. She doesn't need that expensive moisturizer, no longer believing its promises.

She joins Vihaan on the couch where he's stretched out and looking rather haggard. She's amused that he's wearing his unwavering tennis whites as if they were prescribed by a religious practice. She's only seen him in clothes of another color when he's at breakfast in his pajamas or on the few occasions when the group has dressed up for dinner.

Not wanting to hurt him further by touching his bad leg, she volunteers to massage his good one. His skin is toasty, the hair on it silky, his smell musky in an attractive way. This touch sparks more than that she feels at folk dancing or that she shares with Pearl, with whom she often holds hands. She kneads gently.

She remembers when she and Vihaan had been in college together. They were both early risers and chatted together over coffee under the shade of the backyard live oak, the twists and turns of its branches following their own logic. Though there was nothing overtly flirtatious about the times Doris spent with Vihaan, she looked forward to them and was miffed when Vihaan got together with Rose. He was no longer available for her and had become seemingly uninterested in the early morning talks, and he didn't mention the change. That was when she first decided to stop thinking about finding a special someone and started concentrating on areas of her life in which she felt more control. Thus the decades flew past with a few friends with benefits and lots of spells without them until her husband, Howard, surprised her.

Trying to ward off any more nightmares, she lies in bed and pictures stroking Vihaan's leg as if it were a friendly pet. The picture morphs into an image of her head on Howard's chest, his fingers running through her hair. She'd told herself back then to stop worrying about what she needed to do the next day and to savor his presence, to have it for the future when the opportunity might be gone, as it is now.

Pearl is pissed, her lips pursed, scowling. "You're so busy with David and Vihaan these days." Agitated, she nods a dozen times in quick succession as if compelled by a ritual.

"You don't ask me to do things these days," Doris says.

"You seem too busy. And you don't ask me."

"Okay, I'm asking you. What do you want to do?"

"I'll let you know if I think of something," Pearl says and walks away.

Doris doesn't remember them ever arguing, maybe because their friendship was a clear favorite. Pearl had never had to share Doris with Doris's other favorites since they lived halfway across the country from each other when Doris was married. It had been easier back then for Pearl to express happiness that Doris had found a companion, back when it was more abstract to Pearl.

Doris tells herself that she's too old for Pearl's emotional shenanigans. Whether the sparks with David and Vihaan are also nonsense troubles her for a fleeting moment. She'd had so many years of heaviness with her parents' needs as they spiraled down that she welcomes whatever levity, whatever breeze, she can find.

At dinner, Doris catches Pearl staring at her, and she's tempted to stare her down but resists. Pearl's usually a hearty eater, but she just pushes her food around her plate. Not feeling cooled down enough, Doris decides to wait until tomorrow to try to talk to Pearl.

After dinner, Doris knocks on David's door. He's going to try out folk dancing tonight.

"What if I zig when everyone's zagging?" he asks.

"We toss you out."

Several fellow dancers ask if David is her son.

Doris loves that every Saturday night she gets to skip forward and back, round and round, dancing through the upheld arms of the others. She's holding David's hand, and he's grinning, his glasses sliding down his nose, causing him to drop her hand now and then to push them back up. Her foot's a bit sore from his treading on it a few times, but nothing serious. She no longer wears wispy sandals to dance, as she had in years past, but instead has on a sturdy pair of red Chuck Taylors.

A step in one of the dances requires a hop, and Doris pictures Vihaan hopping back and forth from the bathroom and his room.

Back in San Diego, shortly after Howard died, Doris pulled herself out of bed where, other than work, she spent most waking hours. She told herself she'd go to the dance and gave herself permission to leave if it got too sad. There, she could be with others and not feel pressure to talk. Though her inner dialogue was constant, she had little to say. During the breaks, she'd locked herself in a bathroom stall and sat with the lid down, her face in her hands, the tears leaking through.

Back to the present, to the flow, to the shine on the dancers' faces, the rhythm. Here is freedom as she knows it, a defiance of gravity.

"You survived," Doris says to David when they're in the car.

"I can see the charms." He taps on the steering wheel, playing a drum.

Their hug goodnight is their first hug, not too tight, not too loose. The moonlight tower shines in the background, and Ginger Rogers follows Doris home, curling up on the porch as Doris goes in.

"How was it?" Vihaan calls from the living room couch. "Could you have danced all night?"

Doris settles into the chair next to the couch and slips off her shoes, wiggles her toes. "Not without paying for it tomorrow. How's the knee?"

"Vociferous. Will you show me a dance?" He sits up gingerly.

She pushes the coffee table back, and in the space she creates, she takes Vihaan's hand and does slow, slow, quick, quick steps. She starts to duck under his arm but feels her back protesting. When she was young, she was an ace limbo player, bending backward with smooth assurance.

He applauds, and she curtsies. He catches her hand again, and they stay with fingers interlaced until she lets go.

Early the next morning, she finds him back on the sofa. "How about we go sit by the tree?" she asks. "I'll bring us coffee, and you can get some fresh air."

After he's made his effortful way to the backyard and lowered himself with care into a chair, he asks, "Do you remember when we used to do this in the old days?"

"Fondly." She's pleased the memory isn't hers alone.

Pearl is not at the breakfast table, so Doris fills a cup of coffee with a splash of half-and-half as Pearl prefers, and she knocks on her door. "Special delivery," she says. She's nervous, hoping Pearl won't have those flashing eyes this morning.

At Pearl's beckoning, she enters the room, which smells like baby powder and the tea rose perfume Pearl wears. Pearl's eyes are bleary, her hair a fine corona. "Thank you," she says, sitting up and scooting over to create room for Doris to sit.

"I don't know what to do," Doris says.

Pearl blows so hard on the coffee that it trickles over the over the lip of the cup, and she wipes it with the back of her hand. She says, "I want … I wanted …"

Doris waits. Pearl's bedside table is dusty in the dim light. Pearl says softly, "I thought that maybe you and I …"

Doris shifts, and that seems to cause a shift in Pearl. "Oh, I don't know. Never mind," Pearl says.

Doris isn't sure she wants to know what Pearl feels. Maybe she doesn't want Pearl to unburden herself in a way that Doris would feel obliged to acknowledge or even take on the burden. Still, this is her old friend, and she needs to muster up something. "Want to go on a walk after breakfast?"

"That works," Pearl says.

On the walk, Doris offers a prompt for improv. "I've just landed on Earth, and I see by your yellow leg coverings that you can give me a tour of this place." She gestures toward the live oaks, the pecans, the prickly pears, the million-dollar bungalows.

"Yes, and …" Pearl says, adhering to the improv golden rule of agreement. She explains the scenery and the peculiar lives of the Earthlings as they stroll down the street, trying to see the givens through alien eyes. Pearl is walking with a shuffle as if she can't pick up her feet or she's afraid of a fall. That's new.

Doris used to see Pearl as a guide for living a fulfilled single life, a guide for meaningful pursuits, a guide for compassion. First with Doris's marriage and now her growing warmth with David and Vihaan, she has veered from the path they share. She feels both defiant and disloyal, and she wants to hide both feelings from Pearl to protect them both.

Pearl suggests they head home.

Vihaan is not on the couch, and he's not in the bathroom taking his lengthy shower. Vihaan's bedroom door is cracked open, and he lies on his side, eyes open. Doris raps on the door.

"Doris," he says, his voice fond.

"Trying to nap?" She hasn't been in his bedroom before. Like the rest of them, except Tomás and Ellen, he has a single bed. The bed and bedding, the desk, the chair, all are white. She takes her time looking at the pictures of Rose and of his son on his desk. In the pictures, they have not grown older.

"It's not a good day," he says.

"Any special reason?"

"Emptiness. I don't know what to do without tennis. Why did I invest so much in it? I don't know how to spread out."

"Tell me more," she says. The minimalist desk chair is far from comfortable, but Doris tries to believe in discomfort for a worthy cause.

"I've thought that when I leave this world, it will be when I'm decrepit but on the court, hobbling to and fro before I gracefully collapse." He shifts and winces.

"I wonder if a good death is a fantasy," Doris says.

"I'm glad we can be morbid together."

They've spent a lot of time lately with him prostrate, she upright, as if they were doing old-fashioned therapy, except they make eye contact. Rather nice eye contact with Vihaan's big pupils imbibing the light.

"How do you want to die?" Vihaan asks.

"Neatly." Doris laughs. "I don't know." She can't know whether her parents' deaths, when they were wasted by dementia, had been better than clear-headed death.

"If you're ever laid up, Doris, and I don't have a bum knee, can I sit with you?"

"If you have a bum knee, we'll figure out a way we can both lie down."

Vihaan smiles, maybe at the prospect.

Awake late, she envisions how she escaped the wildfire, everything she needed, not everything she wanted, thrown into her Toyota. Her mind skips as quickly as she can make it over the stop-and-go traffic on the way to L.A., her not giving a flip if anyone saw her during a lull pull down her pants and pee into a wide-mouthed pickle jar she'd brought along just in case. The jar of peanuts she was trying to devour as she drove fell to the passenger side floor, and during another forced stop, she scooped them up, swallowed them with a side of lint.

Enough of that. She wants to dwell on the time she spent taking shelter at her friends' house in L.A. Like Vihaan, the friends favored the color white for their interior walls, for their bathrooms, for their bedding. In the early mornings, they'd go out to the backyard orange trees and pick a few. They sprawled on deck chairs and ate the fruit, juice running down their hands and chins. The sky was hazy, but Doris couldn't smell smoke. The birds did their call and response.

The man in the couple, a film historian, planned nightly screenings, an undeclared healing program for Doris. He wanted to share his enthusiasm and esoterica. The fare featured screwball comedies brimming with witty banter, a temporary salve for Doris's rumination. On weekend afternoons, they played wiffle ball, Doris rarely connecting with the ball.

At night, she hugged the spare pillow, breathed in the silk lavender sachet her friends had gifted her. She wrote a letter to Howard describing what had happened and detailing the times when she missed him the most, then she wrote his tender response.

Before she'd moved back into West House, she'd found the folded love letters at the bottom of her purse, the corners of the paper shredded with wear and tear from her dipping into her purse for her wallet, her keys, her phone, all the necessities.

Her stomach rumbles. What is she hungry for? Whatever it is, it can wait until morning.

Chapter 8: Anew

Tomás has no place to put the finished-for-now La Sagrada Familia if he wants to be able to do other projects in his and Ellen's room. Already, they each have a project table on opposite sides of their bed, and they have to turn sideways and sashay to make their way through the narrow passages. When the housemates spent the night with him, it was even more of a challenge.

Each inch of the house and the garage isn't up for negotiation the way space was when he and Ellen had their own place. This substantial Familia would take up half the dining table, not as easy to house as a painting. He considers whether he could suspend Familia from the ceiling like a mobile, but the sculpture is bulbous rather than slim.

Now that he's charmed by the third dimension but needs to conserve space, he wonders if it's too late to become a miniaturist, to construct a tiny Chrysler building or miniature busts of his housemates or his kids. Perhaps his eyes and fine motor skills wouldn't be up to par. Hours fly by as he looks online at the insides of Fabergé eggs, at exquisite dollhouse furniture, and at 2-inch by 2-inch by 2-inch coral reefs and rain forests.

He googles whether lacemakers, with their eyes for the smallest details, go blind. It is indeed a myth, and he even finds a story about a group of blind lacemakers, which cheers him. The cameos of his housemates that he'd painted on leaves are quite small, and that gives him another sprig of hope that he could go a lot smaller. Meanwhile, he's dormant artistically, letting Familia rest heavily on his worktable.

He stands over the sculpture and runs a careful finger over the details. Since the whole endeavor has meant taking vast liberties, he secularized Gaudi's three monumental façades. Gaudi had represented in one Christ's birth; in the second, his passion, death, and resurrection; and in the third, his glory. To one side of the building, Tomás super-glued a brown baby he'd sculpted from modeling clay; on another he's affixed a foil heart; and for glory, he's fashioned a spiky sun out of sliced and painted plain wood chopsticks.

He used to have a gallerist in Dallas who represented his work, but she tanked years ago, and he was unable to find representation after that. That had been a blow. He wonders what the gallerist is doing these days and what she would think of his veering away from his solemn abstracts, which became boring even to him. By the time he and Ellen left Dallas for West House, he'd emptied his studio of the unsold works, giving them to the friends, family, and silent auctions that had at least acted interested. He'd saved one that had been a favorite long ago. Ellen had wanted him to rent a storage unit while he decided what to do with the paintings, but he was ready to travel lightly and inexpensively.

He and Ellen once talked about which sense they'd miss most, and they agreed that going blind would be the hardest. Lately, he's been hiding from her his new obsession with losing his sight, despite his wonderful cataract surgery. He's superstitious that if he says aloud how much of his brain space these fears are taking, he'll be opening a door for descending darkness, daring it to devour him. Meanwhile, the intrusive thoughts are like a dog barking in a neighbor's yard. Just when you think the dog has gone inside to relax, it starts another round.

In the last years of his mother's life, macular degeneration ate up her vision. She was a trouper, embracing audio books and *Jeopardy* without the visuals, and she sat for hours in the living room in her paisley La-Z-Boy with the radio blasting—her hearing not so hot either. The El Paso Lighthouse had visited her and provided numerous assistive devices. He doubts he could be as gracious as his mother was with her loss.

She and his father refused to talk about dying with any of their children and seemingly with each other, despite gentle prodding from the mystified, tiptoeing kids. Maybe his parents were superstitious too, or maybe even in their octogenarian years, they'd been sure death was for other people, just as he is now.

He wakes up without an alarm at 3 a.m., scoops up his sunglasses, and heads first to the bright lights in the bathroom. There he lets his pupils dilate before snapping off the light. Donning the sunglasses and stepping out of the bathroom, he finds navigating through the dark house daunting. He stabs himself in the crotch with a table corner and can't stifle his loud "Shit!" as he doubles over. When he can breathe again, he's relieved that no one seems to have heard him, or if someone did, he's glad that person felt no need to investigate.

He slips back into bed, and Ellen shifts, tugs to her side all the covers. If he tugs back, she might wake up and sigh in irritation. Better to be cold. They have a delicate balance right now, a peace, and he feels the need to prevent grievances, even small ones, so they don't pile up and come tumbling down.

It's been less than a year since he's had his eyes examined, so unless he invents a problem, insurance won't cover another anxious but, he hopes, reassuring visit. Damn.

"What are you staring at, Tomás?" Barry asks as the group sits together eating their lunch salads.

"Just thinking." He's trying to drink in Barry's porous skin, each crease in Barry's neck—Tomás counts seven of them—the rosy tip of his nose, his still-dark eyelashes and arched brows. The color of Barry's silky shirt is cerulean, as refreshing as a swig of cold water.

To be less creepy, Tomás dons a placid smile. He will drink in these friends' faces one by one. He'll do that as a ritual during each meal, the way Doris tries to eat with her nondominant hand because she's heard that it's an Alzheimer's preventive.

It's so easy to stop seeing the familiar anew, and that strikes him as dangerous. Still, he wants to avoid the neurosis of that fellow who kept a written record of every minute—tied shoe, boiled water, peed. Likewise, he isn't one of the rare people who remember almost everything they've ever done, a condition called hyperthymesia. He'd just as soon not be able to conjure the exact details of pain in his marriage. He'd prefer to forget the myriad times when he'd fallen short, his too late realized failures of empathy. But if he could have selective late-onset hyperthymesia, he might not be as devastated if he lost his sight.

"Are you okay?" Ellen asks him.

He nods and distracts from her concern by giving his attention to the reflective silver of the utensils, the sphere of cherry tomato, the astounding symmetry of a sliced hard-boiled egg.

After dinner, he takes pictures of his Sagrada Familia from a number of angles. He crops, adjusts the brightness and contrast, tries filters, but none of the pictures captures the grain of the egg cartoons, the delicate filigree of the leaves.

Tomás knows his neuroses are unwelcome luxuries. He and the other co-opers masochistically scour the news for real horrors, and one night a week, they send protest emails to the powers that be. This month, their pleas are about the scores of tiny kids wrenched from their migrating families, warehoused in pitiful conditions, denied hugs from their temporary guardians. When it came to bad news, near and far, he used to be better at filtering, compartmentalizing. When it comes to pictures of weeping children at crowded detention centers, he has a photographic memory.

A temporary antidote: binging on color. It's November, and although Austin is no Vermont, he takes long strolls to set his eyes on the vermillion, ochre, tangerine leaves. He walks so much that he develops blisters, but he just applies foot plasters and keeps up his rambles.

When he was younger and had a crisis of faith about whether he was suited to keep teaching young people how to paint year after year, he'd considered what it would be like to be a postal carrier. He'd get to walk all day for a living, see people's houses and yards, get barked at but carry kibble in his pocket. To hell with the uniform and Dallas summers, the rhythm and time to muse appealed.

He persuades Barry and Ellen to walk to the paint store with him, just to look. They welcome the suggested outing without questioning his motives. The store clerk indulges him when he asks to take one of each card with paint chip samples. He's known about the seemingly infinite gradations in color, color theory, and the color wheel, but collecting these is like collecting menus from favorite restaurants.

"I love the names," he says to Ellen and Barry. "Parakeet, seafoam, bay leaf."

They peer at the shades of brown. "Your eyes are carob," Ellen says to Tomás.

"Yours are walnut," he responds.

Tomás says to Barry, "I think yours are tawny."

"I'd say root beer," says Ellen.

"Perla," he says.

"I want to show you my last life," she says.

She hands him her phone and gives him a tour of her city through photos she took. Here's her library and the kids whom she had permission to photograph mugging for the camera or serious with hands folded together. Here's the art deco Paterson Building with what looks like a belt of gold-painted masonry crowns. Here are Perla's friends in her compact living room, some on folding chairs, raising glasses of sparkling wine. Here's an extreme close-up of a bunch of unwashed leeks that she'd hung in her Flint bathroom as a pun.

He shuffles through his color cards, and together they identify the leeks' shades of green and white, the shade of brown in the finest dusting of dirt, and that rubber band holding the leeks together is definitely violet.

"These were taken on your phone?" he asks. "You have an eye. Really."

Perla grins, and he takes in her salt-and-pepper braid, her pouchy full cheeks, the pale pink rimming her eyes, the grooves across her forehead. She is lovely. "Off to work," she says, nodding.

His roommates keep unveiling facets. It had been dangerous to bank on reuniting, to count on giving and taking with these friends who until recently had lived far away. Of course, they are a select group; some former co-opers weren't invited to this new community or weren't interested. Though this cohabitation, the dependence on Barry's kindness, is scary, a huge adjustment, if he and Ellen had kept rattling around in their former house by themselves, their kids long gone, who knows what might have happened. His housemates are a buffer, absorbing Ellen's ambivalence. While he wants her to be fulfilled, theoretically, he hopes she makes the best of being stuck with him. He loves the healthier, less brittle Ellen, his late-late bloomer, more than he ever loved her. She kisses him more now, runs her hand over his stubbled head, shows him what she's been working on, whereas when he used to ask her how her day had been, she'd said, "Fine. Not much to report. How about you?"

Before they'd moved back to x Austin, he'd FaceTimed his daughter Luz, who lives in Cleveland. She'd sat her usual way, cross-legged on her sofa, one of his paintings behind her, her wine glass within reach, her dog on her lap. She led with her chin, and she was cupping it now.

She said, "You know, you could live near me. You're not getting younger."

"No kidding. I don't think Mom would go for that."

Luz's face tightened. "It doesn't have to be with Mom."

He moved back, the chair legs scraping the floor. "What makes you think it wouldn't be?"

"Nothing," she'd said and launched into a non sequitur about one of her students never having eaten eggplant. She'd always requested Tomás's Japanese eggplant with ginger and miso whenever she was visiting.

She and his son Ernesto must have conferred because soon thereafter, Tomás got a text from him, asking if he might be interested in a studio apartment in the building where Ernesto and his wife lived. The apartment would have been too small to fit both Tomás and Ellen. "Are you suffering from the empty nest?" Tomás texted back. Ernesto said no, that it was just an idea. "We're good here, but thank you," Tomás wrote.

He's never recounted these conversations to Ellen. He still wonders if she put the kids up to this or whether the kids had decided, as they'd occasionally hinted before, that Tomás might be better off without their mother. They'd complained to him about how little she ate, how she accepted their affection with her hands by her side. Maybe somehow they knew about her infidelity, though certainly neither Tomás nor Ellen would ever burden them with that information.

Tomás watches Perla's sturdy back, her braid a subtle metronome, as she walks away. He stands up, tries to touch his toes. Not even close. The challenge at his age is to exercise but not hurt himself. In the backyard, he alternates between gazing at his surroundings and closing his eyes, enjoying the crimson impression on the back of his eyelids. He hears a plane fly low overhead, the semi-feral cats playing in the crunchy leaves that have piled up, then a susurrus from an unknown source. Tomorrow, he and Ellen are on yard duty.

She's wearing her Kermit-green gardening gloves, and she's the raker, he's the bagger. Four bags full, and they've barely made a dent. He turns around, and she's lying on the ground, rolling back and forth. At first, he thinks something is wrong with her, but she says, "Come on in. The water's fine." He joins her on the ground, and after rolling around for a while, they both lie on their backs, holding hands. "I'm cold," she says, and he holds her to warm her up. He grooms her by picking the leaves out of her hair. She presses her face to his chest.

"You've been very patient with me," she says.

He doesn't know if she's been patient with him since she hides a lot, or at least she used to. He does know that she's not so patient with herself, scoffing when she drops something or scolding herself aloud with a "What are you doing?" when she makes a mistake.

"And you've been forgiving," she says.

He has been. "Do you need to forgive me?" he asks.

"Maybe. I wanted you to talk more about my eating. You didn't know about the other … stuff."

He had talked to her about the eating, and she always countered with, "I've got it under control." He could see no point in bringing up his past expressions of concern now.

Pushing up with much effort from all fours, they're back on their feet. She brushes leaves off his sweater and his backside. He takes in the long slide of her nose, her dove gray pixie cut mussed from rolling around. They lean against their mascot oak.

His inner alarm has woken him up again at 3 a.m. He sighs. Sagrada Familia lies in wait on the table, a shade of matte gunmetal in the darkness. The urgency to do something with it, make room for experiments in miniature, feels more pressing.

He's back to picturing the kids in the migrant detention center. They have no guarantee of a bed, and in one photo he saw, they lie crowded on the concrete floor, each wrapped in the kind of Mylar blanket given to runners at the end of a marathon, as they try to sleep with the lights on.

His legs itch to move, and he rises. In the bright light of the bathroom, he takes off his T-shirt and wraps it around his head as a blindfold. He stumbles around the house until he's drunk with exhaustion and lies down on the thin living room rug, his head under the coffee table.

He awakes when someone calls his name. He can't see who it is. Something is around his head, and his face is damp. He tears off the T-shirt, then shades his eyes from the bright light. Those are Jane's knobby ankles, her feet snug in turquoise terry cloth slippers. Someone else thumps into the room and stands next to Jane. Vihaan, in his pristine sneakers.

"What are you doing, buddy?" Vihaan says.

"I don't know." He is too ashamed to explain. Will it be worse if they think he's drunk or demented or neurotic? He doesn't need to decide now. He tries to sit up but bumps his head hard on the underside of the coffee table.

Before they can express their concern to Ellen, he extracts himself from under the table and hauls himself up. His legs are cramping.

"Thank you. I need to go talk to Ellen."

"Glad you're okay," says Jane.

Ellen is in their bedroom, sitting up in bed, wearing her crimson robe and peeling a mandarin orange. "Want to share?" she asks, holding out half of it.

He nods and sits next to her. He savors each orange section, takes the peels from Ellen's plate and rubs them on his inner wrists as if they were cologne, which he inhales deeply.

"I want to share something else with you."

"Please do."

He confesses his obsession about losing his sight and finds himself tearing up.

"Oh, sweetie. You've been carrying that around by yourself. How can I help?"

"I'm going to think what I think, but it's good to unburden." He thinks of how he was the preferred parent to untangle Luz's snarled hair when she was little. He had a patient, gentle touch. Now Ellen, she of the walnut brown eyes, could keep him company as he combs out the snarls in his mind.

"I'm worried about the kids," he says.

"What kids?" She sniffs his wrists.

"Homeless kids, scared kids, scarred kids."

She scans his troubled face. "What about the grownups?"

"That's too much."

"Okay, you worry about the kids. I'll worry about the grownups." She smooths his brow.

"Worrying is useless. We used to donate." His face feels itchy, and he scratches at it. The living room rug he'd slept on had irritated his skin.

"We're conserving our money now," Ellen says. "But what about giving time?"

"That we've got," he says. Volunteering would cut into his ruminating time. Good. He experiments with a nibble of mandarin rind. Bitter, but he knew that already.

When Ellen leaves the room, he makes himself look up what's known about macular degeneration, research he's avoided. Yes, in some cases, it's inheritable; in others, not.

It's time for breakfast and for Tomás to explain why he was sprawled under the coffee table this morning. He's decided it's preferable to fess up rather than have Jane and Vihaan and whomever they might have told think he's more out of it than he is. Doris has made breakfast tacos, and they pass around the salsa.

He clears his throat. "I'd like to tell y'all about an issue I've been having."

They wait.

He explains why he was practicing being unable to see. "It's like a new tic."

"I was wondering why you've been staring at us during meals," Vihaan says.

Barry says, "Show of hands. Who here isn't anxious sometimes?"

Ellen's hand shoots up, then falls down. "Just kidding," she says.

He rests Sagrada Familia on the bed's comforter and tidies his desk. He has a spool of thin wire for the body of Austin's moonlight towers, faux seed pearls from a bracelet Ellen gave him to use as tiny light bulbs. His moonlight tower will be to scale and smaller than his palm.

He overhears Neighbor David and Barry in the kitchen, making tarte Tatin. Because he likes the ambient noise, he opens his door wider just as David is passing through the hallway.

"May I ask what that is?" David says, gesturing toward Tomás's sculpture.

"Come on in," he says. "I'll introduce you."

David appreciates the details.

"Do you have room for it?" Tomás asks. "It needs a new home."

"Really?"

Tomás nods. "No pressure," he says.

"I can think of a place for it, and I'd love to have it." David wipes his hands on his jeans. His eyes are cornflower. "Are you sure?"

"Sure, I'm sure." The scent of cinnamon and apples wafts toward them.

"But why are you saying goodbye to it?"

"Freeing up space." They plan for David to finish his baking and come back when he's dusted the space where the sculpture will take up residence.

Meanwhile, Tomás asks Perla to take pictures of La Familia. As he suspected, she does the work justice, seeing it in a way he couldn't. After David takes the sculpture, Tomás confronts the mostly empty space on his table. Once again, he shuffles through his deck of color samples, the riches.

Chapter 9: Traveler

"This really is quite treatable."

Tomás listens to the doctor describing Ellen's options, and he jots down the pros and cons of each treatment, while Ellen half-hears, her mind drifting to her friend Sally in Dallas who'd died from breast cancer.

"We've caught this …"

That's reassuring, but she's back in Sally's airless bedroom, offering to open the curtains, and Sally protesting. "I can't take it." The light? The suffering?

"Ellen," Tomás says. "Do you have questions?"

"What would you recommend?" she asks, her voice light, as if the answer were only as consequential as that asked to a server at a restaurant. She expects the doctor to hedge and to sum up what she's already said. She holds her breath.

The doctor wheels her chair closer. "How attached are you to that breast?"

Refreshingly straightforward. "Now, that's a good question," she says. She studies the wood laminate floor, musing about how medical offices are homier than they used to be.

"No need to decide today," the doctor says. "But soon."

Last week her breasts were just there, stuffed in a bra she'd chosen for comfort over style, succumbing to gravity in a way that would have bothered her when she was younger. As she and

Tomás pass through the oncology waiting area, a few people look up from their phones or *People*. Though Ellen doesn't know at which stage of the journey these folks are, she smiles and nods at each one of them. She likes the term "fellow traveler" and thinks it's a pity when it's used as a pejorative. Her legs tremble, and the air smells like burnt hair.

In the car, as Tomás drives, she feels her left breast, the cancerous one. Her breast weighs more than it did last week when the doctor had called with the news. She tries to feel her heartbeat, but it's gone into hiding. At a stoplight, Tomás takes her hand and squeezes it, she squeezes back, and they release when the light changes. On her lap is the folder the doctor gave them, stuffed with metanalyses, information about support groups, exercise and nutrition recommendations. The blissfully not-pink folder is smooth, and she pets it, missing Fred the Cat, who could be cajoled onto her lap when Jane was out grocery shopping or in the shower.

At home, the housemates are gathered in the living room, a tentative-looking greeting committee. She's touched.

"Do you want to talk about it?" Barry asks.

Her first thought is that she doesn't want to burden them because, surely, they'd had enough already of her impositions. Her second thought is that she doesn't want them to burden her with their concern. Her third thought is that in her past efforts to escape burdening or being burdened, she was hiding, and that was tiring, lonely.

"I'll do my best," she says.

Under Vihaan's usual diplomatically neutral expression, Ellen detects a wisp of fear. Of course, his Rose died from breast cancer.

"I've got options," Ellen says. "I'm lucky that way." Though she was only half-hearing what the doctor said at the time, in a delayed reaction, she's absorbed the broad strokes of her choices and describes them, with murmurs of encouragement from the group. "And now," she says, "I've got to collapse."

Though it's not his turn to cook tonight, Barry makes one of Ellen's favorites, chicken piccata with radicchio salad on the side.

After dinner, in the privacy of the bedroom, she studies the metanalyses until her head swims. Chemo, radiation, lumpectomy, mastectomy—matter-of-fact words for exhausting possibilities. Poisoning, burning, slicing, scooping, emptying—all for the good.

Tomás offers to share the news with the kids, but she wants to do it herself. He's often swooped in, been swifter to talk and connect with them, he the jovial light, she the icy shadow. They call her by her first name, while they call Tomás "Papi." When Vihaan told her about the gulf between his son and him, Ellen recognized the feelings.

After she tells the kids, of course she hopes they'll be supportive of Tomás even if they decide to maintain the distance they've been keeping from her. She feels guilty about all the "in sickness" aspects of their marriage Tomás has had to endure already.

How attached is she to her breast? Enough to feel as though losing it would be an amputation.

She's never asked Vihaan about the kind of treatment his wife got. Her friend Sally had undergone chemo and radiation but hesitated to get surgery because she was single and hoped that intact breasts would make a future relationship easier. Later, she thanked Ellen for being the only person who didn't insist that Sally was going to get through this. "I'm so sick of people telling me I'm not going to die," she'd said.

Ellen knows that whatever she does, she has no guarantees.

As they're going to sleep, Tomás whispers, "I'm here. I'll be here." She hugs him fiercely.

***

Ellen asks the women in the household to meet with her. They gather in the backyard, where it's private enough. A new blanket of leaves covers the grass. Ellen had felt so carefree when she and Tomás rolled around in the leaves. When Ginger Rogers hops on Jane's lap, Ellen leans over and pets her.

"What do you feel about your breasts?" she asks her friends.

Silence.

Jane says, "I'd feel differently about them if I were in your situation, but right now they feel like my ears. They stick out."

"Don't say anything to be nice," Ellen says. "I don't want nice."

"I'm kind of fond of them," Doris ventures. "But they were a nuisance when I used to jog."

Pearl purses her lips, then nods. "Frankly, I keep getting a rash under mine. And I don't like when women call them 'the girls.'"

It's a relief to laugh, but the levity evaporates just like that. "Are you being nice?" Ellen asks, her foot tapping.

"What's more important today is how you feel about your breasts," Doris says.

She sighs. "Today, I don't know." She's never turned to the women before.

Jane says, "What's important is how you feel about having cancer."

"Can I get back to you on that?" she says. An emergency vehicle sounds its alarm on a nearby street. Someone is in distress. How many someones all over their city? When the noise dies down, she says, "I just wish I hadn't microwaved in plastic."

The other women don't smile. Doris says, "I wasn't there for Vihaan and Rose, but I can be for you."

"I second that," Jane says.

Pearl says, "Me too." She clears her throat. "I mean, I as well."

Ellen points out a cardinal wearing its scarlet coat, perched in a tree, and she hums silently, "I'll Fly Away." Oh, wait, that hymn is about dying. She switches to "Amazing Grace."

Ginger the cat is mesmerized by the cardinal. For winter, it's a warm day, and when Ellen lowers her face toward the cat, she sees how the sun glosses the cat's worn coat, and she can smell the pleasant scent of the sun burnishing the cat's fur.

"Thank you," she says to her friends. She stares at the mascot oak, as if it holds answers.

She's never apologized to her kids for checking out, for being so uptight, and she's sure they have unaired grievances. Though she's been more engaged with them these past few years, initiating conversations, asking more questions about their lives, their responses are stilted and spare. She understands why they're guarded.

She texts them, asking to arrange a time to talk. After a few days, Luz responds first, suggesting a phone call rather than FaceTime.

Ellen was planning on sharing the cancer news, but instead she finds herself saying, "I'm sorry for not being there for you in the way I could have."

"It's okay," Luz says.

She waits and wonders if that's Luz's request to move on, as if they need to keep trying to glide over the rubble.

Luz says, "Well, actually maybe it's not okay. Why are you apologizing now?"

She hadn't planned on using her cancer to fast-forward to a better place with the kids, but here she is. "I have a spot of cancer," she says.

"I'm sorry."

A lull, no questions. Ellen might be trying to water a withered plant that's long past watering, the water beading up on the dry soil instead of being absorbed. "I wish you would unload on me," she says. "I can take your anger." She's ready for whatever. Maybe.

"Maybe anger turns to apathy."

She wants to protest, "I've changed!" She knows she needs instead to validate Luz's feelings, or lack thereof, but that's still a foreign language for her, a nakedness. She's stumbling until she utters, "I understand."

"I'm not sure you do."

"I want to understand." Apathy and anger, ice and storms, ruled the climate she'd tried to keep subterranean for so long.

"I know how you are isn't about me or Ernesto or Papi. But you can't just suddenly show up and expect a warm welcome."

Ellen lets herself hope that Luz says that with anger. Anger's a sign of life.

"I'll be there for Papi," Luz says, before she severs the call.

"I'm trying," Ellen says aloud, aware of both senses of the word.

She finds Tomás with Vihaan in the living room speaking in hushed tones. Maybe they're talking about her and about Rose. She imagines the pressure on Rose to keep rallying, to exhaust any means of treatment, quantity of life over quality. But Ellen doesn't know how Rose's illness unfolded, and she's not ready to hear. She already has her friend Sally rising up from the dead, and she forces herself to tear her remembrances away from Sally retching and writhing to replace them with memories of Sally glowing as she and Ellen sipped martinis at a swanky bar. Ellen had listened raptly as Sally recounted the trip she'd just taken to Cinque Terre. Ellen had been both envious of and delighted by Sally's freedom. "We'll go there someday," Sally said, "Just you and me. Or Costa Rica or Japan." Although Sally invited her along each time she had an international adventure, Ellen declined, explaining that she didn't have the money or the time.

"Don't want to interrupt," Ellen says to Tomás and Vihaan.

In the bedroom, she sits for many minutes over a blank sketchpad. Nothing comes.

After more discussions with the oncologist and Tomás, Ellen decides to say goodbye to the breast that threatens to rob her of more than it has already. After that, the oncologist will determine whether chemo or radiation is necessary.

Now she has to choose what to do with the empty breast. For reconstruction, she can have an implant or move fat or muscle into the breast. The surgeon leaves her and Tomás alone with a catalog of the different options, photos of real women.

"I don't care," she says, slumping, her usual good posture too much of an effort. Her hunching hides her chest as if protecting her from invisible blows. She flips through the pages until she arrives at a photo of a woman who chose to go flat, to forego reconstruction. According to the text under the photo, the woman chose an incision that's called the "gull wing."

"Luz told me," Ernesto says when he calls. "That sucks."

She hears tinkling music in the background. "Did she tell you I apologized for not being much of a mother?"

Ernesto clears his throat. "Sofia and the kids send love."

"Is there anything you need to get off your chest?" She imagines that protective smile of his and the way his eyes dart away from hers.

"The past is the past. You've been a good *abuela*."

"I appreciate that." She was able to play with the grandkids, hold them close, and support their dreams. With Luz and

Ernesto, they would share their fantasies at the dinner table, Tomás the yes man, she the silent voice of caution, not wanting them to be disappointed if things didn't work out the way they wished. By the time the grandkids came around, she trusted them, could see them as their own people rather than as her mystifying extensions.

"Tell me about you," Ellen says. She lies down and bathes in his news.

When her friend Sally had urged her to try harder to thaw with the kids, Ellen had deflected, swallowing her urge to tell Sally to butt out. "I wish they could know the you that I know," Sally had said.

Tomás is off at a training to volunteer at the children's shelter. He got on that quickly, while Ellen has shelved the idea of volunteering until she's in a better place.

Jane asks to speak to Ellen privately. Yesterday it was 80 degrees, today it's 40, so the backyard is out. iPad in hand, Jane comes to Ellen's room and pats the art-table chair, so Ellen perches on it while Jane stands. Hands shaking, Jane opens a tab on the computer to show Ellen a site called "Not Putting on a Shirt."

"Do you want me to leave you with this?" Jane asks.

"I'd like you to stay." She reaches for Jane's hand, and Jane moves closer. Jane's hand quivers as if it has its own rapid heartbeat.

Ellen sifts through the photos and personal stories shared by those farther along their journeys. Some of the women call themselves "flatties."

Ellen feels as if a sturdy and gentle thread is pulling her to sit up straight. "They're free. For now."

Jane says, "That's right."

"I'd be asymmetrical."

Jane ponders that. "I like the word 'unusual.'"

Ellen particularly likes the photos of women who have vivid tattoos over their scars. Dragonfly, hummingbird, peacock, mandala, flowering vine. A cover-up, for sure, but creative. The side where she has the mastectomy will feel both more naked and less naked, she imagines.

Tomás empties the post-surgical drain that trails from where her breast used to be. He marks the notepad where he's keeping track of the times to empty the drain, the times for meds. Ellen needs to sleep and lie there sitting up, so he fluffs and adjusts the pillows wedged behind her and tucks more pillows under her arms. The last time he tended to her this way was when the kids were born.

Luz and Ernesto are staying at Barry's friend Cliff's Airbnb. They take turns sitting by the bed talking about nothing, and Ellen, doped up, drifts in and out.

Once she awakens to find Luz holding her hand, examining her palm as if it had revelations, though Luz is a hardened skeptic.

"I'm still sorry," Ellen says.

"I believe you," Luz replies.

She hears Ernesto holding court in the kitchen; he used to do drama in school and still knows how to project. He's volunteered to make dinner for the group each night. Tonight he brings in a bowl of pho, vivid mint and basil sprinkled over the top.

The kids take her on the walks she's supposed to have, holding her elbow. She can't comfortably stoop to pet Ginger or the other semi-ferals, but Luz and Ernesto do. In the distance a bird calls. "It sounds like it's saying, 'Gee, clean your teeth. Clean your teeth,'" Ellen says. Luz smiles at her as if surprised she has a sense of humor.

A butter-yellow rose in a slender glass vase appears on her art table. Tomás hands her the accompanying card: "Best wishes and love from Vihaan (and Rose)."

The fears of suffering and death that she'd back-burnered to get through this treatment, perhaps just the first treatment, flood her. Because her fears insist on being heard, she takes herself in her mind to the Rothko chapel with its spare, backless benches, the black triptychs that line the walls of the octagonal building. A few of the matte canvasses have warm undercurrents of royal purple or deepest blue. The chapel is windowless. Rothko had wanted a skylight, but the Houston sun might have damaged the art. Recently, the area next to the chapel was vandalized with splashes of white paint and handbills that read, "It's okay to be white." When, in her mind's eye, she's sat on the backless bench for long enough, she exits the chapel and watches the crew that's cleaning up the vandalism. She asks if she can help, and they give her a bucket of soapy water. The crew is just humoring her, but she doesn't mind. A child who resembles her granddaughter when she was younger places a yellow rubber ducky in the soapy water with its iridescent bubbles.

The roommates spell Tomás, taking turns bringing Ellen her meals until she's well enough to sit at the dining table.

Tattoos are expensive, painful, and long term, so Ellen, now several months post-op, rules them out. She locks the bedroom door, takes off her shirt. She's given up on bras because she doesn't want to put a prosthesis in the empty cup. She looks at her chest in the mirror and takes a black Sharpie from a bouquet of them on her art table. She starts drawing on her flat side, a Keith Haring homage with childlike outlines of freefalling bodies, both playful and serious. Her friend Sally, near death, had said she was falling. With broad strokes, Ellen fills in the outlines, yellow, red, purple, brown. Her skin has little sensation. She can lie flat on her back now, so she does and fans a hand over the drawing to help it dry.

When she shows Tomás, he smiles and runs his hand over her picture.

Many showers later, the permanent marker has faded, just a shadow, and one night, Ellen invites Tomás to create the next drawing in what will become a series.

Chapter 10: Glint

Does Barry really need any more friends?

Cliff slows down for him, and they skate side by side. When Cliff turns to talk to him, Barry sees himself reflected and tiny in Cliff's glasses.

He has sprung for sturdy skates. At first, he appreciated the difference between his new skates and the flimsier rental skates, but now he takes the skates for granted.

In the center of the rink, two young men are ice dancing, and Cliff and Barry pause to lean on the rink wall and appreciate. The young men take turns leading and following. They hold hands and rotate faster and faster, their arms the spokes of a wheel, until one man leans back, trusting the other to hold him up, their clasped hands bearing the strain.

"Can you imagine being able to do that?" Cliff says.

"I'm happy watching."

They've spent significant time together only at the rink. In the past, Barry was the one to make the first overture in relationships that had fizzled out, so now he wants to take a wait-and-see approach.

When he'd driven Luz and Ernesto back and forth from the Airbnb cottage in Cliff's backyard, Cliff came out a couple of times and greeted them from the deck. He was barefoot despite the chill, his feet red. Cliff has that kind of flushed skin that looks as if it might be as hot as a radiator. Through the back window of Cliff's house, Barry could see a kitchen island on which sat a bowl of ruby grapefruits, a box of Familia, and a print newspaper. Lining a flowerbed that borders Cliff's back deck, shrimp plants, still green with pink tops, have been toughing out the winter.

The ice-dancing couple twirls to a stop. When Barry and Cliff applaud, the young men face them, holding hands and bowing.

Cliff invites Barry to have a cup of coffee in the rink lounge, and they talk about places they've traveled and where they'd like to go next. Barry doesn't want to travel alone anymore, and he couldn't just treat one of his roommates and not another, so he plays along with Cliff but doesn't imagine he could go anywhere far.

"I want rijsttafel in Jakarta," Cliff says.

"Couscous and tagine in Marrakesh."

"Steak in Buenos Aires."

When Ernesto's daughters were little, he sent them, at Pearl's suggestion, *Oh, the Places You'll Go*. Oh, the places he'd never go. Maybe holding a warm coffee cup in his chilly hands, looking across the table at an appealing man who has a silver five o'clock shadow is enough, at least for today.

One of the older men from the online site reaches out to Barry, and now they're sitting across from each other at a Moroccan restaurant, sharing couscous and tagine. The other man pushes his food around the plate. Lack of vigorous appetite might be a deal-breaker for Barry. Perhaps the other man is nervous, Barry thinks, trying on compassion, as the man rubs his white cloth napkin between his fingers.

Barry has to keep the conversation going, asking questions, to which the other man gives long, winding answers but not returning the questions. It's like in basketball, a player dribbling the ball until the shot clock runs out, never passing it.

He considers polishing off the man's unfinished food and recalls how his hungry siblings would start eating off his plate if he didn't gobble his share quickly enough. When the man starts on grievances against his last partner, Barry gives up the idea of ordering the meskouta orange cake.

Later the man messages Barry, saying, "I think that went well, didn't it?"

Barry shows the message to Ellen, to whom he's given a date report. "What do I say?"

"You're better at this than I am."

"Just 'thanks'? 'Don't think we're a good fit'? 'You don't eat enough and you're boring'?"

"Ouch," says Ellen. She's sketching Barry and asks him to stay still.

He tries not to be caught looking at Ellen's top, but he has yet to get used to the swoop of her remaining breast on one side, the flatness on the other.

After Tomás had brought her home from the hospital, he was wiped out, so he took a nap in Barry's bed while Barry sat on the bed next to the dozing Ellen in her pillow fortress. He'd tried to read a book but ended up just watching her face with its fluttering eyelids, the freckles too many to count, some melted together with age. When they were young, Ellen lay in her crocheted bikini on a towel in the backyard of the co-op, her body oiled with coconut-scented Hawaiian Tropic; her sheets had smelled like coconut.

She turns her sketchpad so Barry can see. "Ugh," Barry says. "The loose skin, the wrinkles, the dark circles under my eyes. How about a little Photoshop, some Autotune?"

Ellen erases a few lines. "Still charming after all these years," she sings. "Why don't you invite Cliff over? You like him."

"Do I need another friend?"

***

When Barry and Cliff walk out of the skating rink, they find freezing rain. It's only four o'clock but dark, with a few blinking streetlamps, a sheen on the macadam. Nearby, a car revs, then does a 360, its brakes squealing before it skids into the back of a parked car. "Oh, shit," Cliff says. A man emerges from the car and leaves a note under the windshield wiper of the car he hit.

Cliff says to Barry, "You shouldn't be driving in this weather. Why don't you come over and wait it out? It'll take us five minutes to walk there slowly."

Arm in arm, they walk and glide to Cliff's place. They leave their wet shoes and socks on the front porch and their skating bags in the front hall. Cliff turns up the heat.

"How about a hot toddy?" he asks Barry as he puts a kettle on.

"Sounds delicious. I'm just going to call the folks at home to let them know what's up." He dials Jane, who always picks up, though it takes her a few rings to steady her hands enough. When he reports that he's at Cliff's house, she says a loud, "Aha! Excellent!" which Barry hopes Cliff can't hear from the kitchen. "I'll stay until it's safer to drive," he says. Jane says how the forecast is for the ice storm to continue until the morning. "You'll get to know each other," she says.

Barry sits in his wet jeans on a towel on the sofa. Cliff offers a pair of sweatpants with an elastic waistband. Barry goes to change in the bedroom and finds the pants a little tight but soft and cozy. Cliff has a king-size bed with a maroon and forest green paisley comforter. The wall opposite the bed is painted the same shade of green as that in the comforter, and Cliff imagines how relaxing it must be to look up groggily from the bed, just before drifting off or just after waking up, to see that placid wall standing guard. The abstracts hung on the wall have the initials CB on the lower right-hand corner, Cliff Baker.

Cliff takes Barry's jeans and throws them in the dryer, and Barry can hear the gentle thump as they circle round. The rain whooshes and ice crystals tap on the windows as they talk and talk and talk. They tell their coming-out stories, their war stories from the height of the AIDS crisis. They bond over their love of Barbara Stanwyck and Django Reinhardt. Another hot toddy and handfuls of pistachios later, Cliff asks if he is hungry. "How about cheese soufflé? I've got a good chèvre."

After Cliff puts the ramekins on a heated cookie sheet in the oven, they wait. "It's so hard to resist opening the oven to see how they're doing."

Strangely for Barry, much as he usually wishes for a sneak peek at the future, he doesn't feel the need to open the oven to see how he and Cliff will turn out.

Barry whisks a vinaigrette for an arugula salad, and they sit to eat. As Barry is oohing and ahhing about the soufflé's lightness, as he takes a final forkful, the lights flicker and go out. He and Cliff go to the front porch and see that the streetlights and other houses' lights are out too.

Cliff has a rechargeable flashlight plugged into the living room wall, and he uses it as he rummages around in a cabinet and finds candles. He spreads them around the dining and living room, creating pockets of wavering orange light.

Cliff prepares a plate of madeleines and champagne grapes, and after carefully lighting the pilot light, he puts on a kettle for tea. Barry likes the way he dips a finger into the cookies crumbs on his plate and licks them off.

"I usually take a bath after dinner," Cliff says. "Dead sea salt."

"Feel free," Barry says. "I could clean up the kitchen."

"Thanks, but don't bother. Would you like to join me in the bath? It's big enough for two."

Barry is stumped, as if Cliff has asked him to translate something written in Greek. He hasn't been naked with someone in years now, hasn't soaked in a bathtub since he lived in New York. "Sure," he says.

He's grateful for the dim forgiving candlelight because he feels clumsy and is reminded of the way gravity has affected his body. The tub is snug, their right thighs resting against each other. They wash each other's feet with peppermint soap.

Cliff says, "I was waiting for you to invite me to something, so I'm glad today gave us an opportunity."

"I was waiting for you."

They crack up, and a wave of bath water splashes onto the bathmat.

The move out of the warm water into the brisk air is painful but softened by the fluffy towel Cliff has set out for Barry. Under the sink, Cliff finds a bag from his dentist that has a fresh toothbrush.

In bed, they whistle Django's "Limehouse Blues." After an ardent kiss, Cliff asks, "Are you good?"

"I'm good. You?"

"Better."

As Cliff blows out the candles, Barry sees Cliff's complexion flushing cinnamon.

Later, Barry is awoken by the lights that are now on, and he moves around the house switching them off. He runs a hand over the forest green wall, and when he snuggles under the covers again, Cliff says, "Thank you." To help himself fall back asleep, Barry pictures the young men ice dancing together, swirling, spinning around and around until they whirl into a pastel blue cone of spun sugar, cotton candy.

Waking up to an empty bed, Barry is disoriented. Then he smiles and pads off to the bathroom to brush his teeth. Following the smell of coffee and the sunlight, he finds Cliff at the dining table, reading a newspaper. They hug, and Cliff runs his hand over Barry's cheek. Barry takes a section of the newspaper, and they read and eat Familia.

Barry needs to get home to give the car to those doing a grocery run today. The ice on the streets and sidewalks has melted, and Cliff offers to walk to Barry's car with him, but he's happy to walk by himself. En route, he appreciates the glint of water before it dries, and he skirts the branches that are casualties of the storm. The sun is the color of the soufflé he ate with Cliff last night. Wind chimes ring like a xylophone, and a smooth gray rabbit tries to keep a low profile on a lawn.

A mushroom medley, sole in saffron sauce. He'd like to cook for Cliff, for his friend, his whatever.

Chapter 11: Unraveling

AFTER HER FRIEND had banked his sperm for Jane, they constructed a contract in which he would have no responsibility for children that might come from the insemination. When Jane was pregnant, her friend moved to Seattle. They'd exchanged holiday cards for several years, then fallen out of touch. Although Amy had been curious to know how she was conceived, she didn't ask many questions about the donor.

Here is his name, a distinctive one, Byron Jamison, in Jane's email. She lets it sit for a day before she opens it. Byron asks how Jane and Amy are, and he updates her on his work and retirement. He and his daughter are planning a cross-country road trip, and he wonders if he could visit Jane in Massachusetts. "I'd love to meet Amy, if she's available. I'm getting older, surprise! I find myself wondering what's happened to people I've cared about."

Jane responds warmly but doesn't mention what happened with Amy. "I'm in Austin now, living with a group of old friends, so unless Texas is part of your journey …"

Byron writes, "As a matter of fact, I want to make it to all the states I've never visited, as well as the ones where I've lived. Texas is on the list of use it or lose it."

Jane and Barry are sharing tea and shortbread in the kitchen. She's pulling at a loose thread at the hem of her sweater, and she knows that if she keeps tugging, it could unravel irreparably. She fetches the kitchen shears and snips off the thread, ties the loose end into a double knot, surprised at her dexterity when the stakes are low. She can do a more solid fix of it later. "Do I tell him about Amy now or when I see him?'

"It might be unkind to spring it on him," Barry says.

He helps her with the wording, and she closes her eyes as she hits the Send button. She's already feeling imposed upon and is tempted to make an excuse to avoid seeing Byron. *Here, let me dump this death on you, and then let me disappear.*

Later that afternoon, the double-knotted thread in her sweater slips through the weave, and Jane allows herself to keep pulling on it until half the sweater is comprised of crimped threads long enough, she imagines, to reach from one end of the house to the other. She leaves the ruined sweater in the backyard so the cat colony or the squirrel brigade or the bird families can use it if they please. It's an ivory sweater, an aged surrender flag.

Byron writes back. He is so sorry. Jane keeps her response to a simple thank you.

Byron has shrunk, his shoulders narrowed, his chest concave. When they were friends back in the day, she'd been drawn to his twinkling eyes, his dimples. Amy had those eyes and dimples too. Byron's daughter, Eve, trails behind him, and Jane is struck by her resemblance to Amy. A wave fills her throat as if she's swallowed scalding water, and the burn radiates out to her fingers and palms.

Byron is looking at her shaking hands, and he grasps them gently in his enveloping ones. He doesn't know that Jane's tremor is beyond circumstantial; the tremor has become a guest that now has no place else to go.

Byron and Eve are staying at Cliff's Airbnb, and Cliff has offered to host dinner for Jane, Barry, and the visitors. Barry makes fajitas, chili con queso, guacamole, nopalitos. All of them except Byron, who says alcohol doesn't agree with him, drink too many mango margaritas, and Jane grows tipsy. She's trying to hold back talking about Amy until there's a more sober, quiet moment. So instead she focuses on Eve, whose life has unfurled as Amy's might have if she'd just taken a different fork in the road or maybe a U-turn. Jane takes bittersweet pleasure in the way Eve is a state congresswoman with a dermatologist wife. Jane looks at videos of Eve's beagles playing in a park.

"I'm going to get a puppy," Jane announces. She feels itchy with love to give to a small, squirming fuzzball.

Barry raises his eyebrows. "Really?" He stares at Jane's empty cocktail glass. "How about some coffee?"

Obviously, adopting a dog is a house decision, not Jane's alone. "I'd like to," she says in a pleading voice. "Or maybe an elderly dog that's down on its luck." She pictures a hound with soulful eyes.

Cliff is clearing dishes, and Barry starts the coffee pot. Surely, Barry has room in his heart for one more stray. She'll work on him later.

After dinner, they sit in the living room, Jane next to Byron on the sofa. "May I?" Byron says, and Jane nods before he takes her hands in his again. What if he had been Amy's other parent? Could the two of them as a tag team have saved her? At first, she'd thrived as a single parent, having Amy all to herself, no one to contradict her parenting. Later, the secrets, the isolation, had been like a case of the emotional bends.

"Tomorrow?" Byron whispers to Jane as they as they hug and say goodnight.

"Amy?" Jane whispers back, and Byron nods.

Jane holds onto Eve a little too long as they say goodnight.

Barry drives her home. "Eve looks a bit like Amy, yes?"

She's afraid that if she says anything, she'll start crying. She should have bought stock in Kleenex. On those lonely trips to Costco after Amy died, no one to partake in the samples of antioxidant mix and samosas with Jane, she stocked up on twelve-packs of Kleenex and giant boxes of berries that inevitably molded in the fridge because the task of rinsing the berries before eating them seemed insurmountable.

At home, Jane takes a handful of blueberries from the crisper and lets the water run over them and her fingers. She pats them dry with a paper towel and stands over the sink eating them one by one.

In the morning, Eve comes over in sweatpants and a hoodie to go play tennis with Vihaan. Byron wants to go for a polar bear swim at Barton Springs, and Jane agrees to accompany him but not to get in the water. First, they sit, clutching their insulated cups of cappuccino, on the gentle slope of yellowed grass bordering the pool.

"This is how she lived in the early years," Jane begins. Again, Byron is holding her hands, keeping them warm. She'd once had a pair of gloves lined with fake rabbit fur, and this is what Byron's hands feel like. "Verve. A number of her teachers whispered to me, 'I'm not supposed to have a favorite, but …' She couldn't tolerate it if you walked ahead of her because she always wanted to lead. She liked to walk on her hands and spin around and stand on her head for long periods of time. She had an imaginary younger brother whom she bossed around and lectured."

"I wish I'd known her," says Byron.

"When she went off to college, she had to work hard for the first time. It scared her. She gave up. She came home and worked as a tech at my clinic, then set her sights on skiing. That's when she had her accident and started the painkillers. I stood outside her room listening once when she was talking to herself. 'You'll never be good enough,' she said, the kind of thing she'd say to her imaginary brother."

He sighs. "Maybe she got it from me, the addictive tendency. My wife left me because I drank too much, which made me drink more. I only stopped because Eve and my son wouldn't talk to me anymore."

"Was all that time when you were drinking wasted?" Jane asks. Surely, Amy had some good times despite her addiction. Didn't she laugh? Didn't she have enthusiasms—coming home from the library with armloads of books, perfecting a flourless cupcake, mountain biking.

"Not wasted," he says. "But it was like sleepwalking a lot of the time. I could still love. I could still function. Eve said the alcohol was a wall. I was muffled. Now I see I was a sieve, time escaping through the holes."

Looking slight in his baggy swim shorts and rashguard, Byron braves the water. He disappears under the surface and pops up, gasping so loudly that Jane can hear him from a distance.

She takes her backpack to the pool locker room. She packed a swimsuit, robe, and towel, just in case.

The cold water is painful, jabbing, making her curl up as if to shield herself. Still, if she could survive the pain she's already survived, this is nothing. She tries an underwater screech, liking how it's muffled. Her body warms, acclimates, given time.

Back at the house, Byron leafs through albums with Amy's photos, so many more taken when Amy was young, of course. The last photo shows Amy napping on the velvet couch, her dark hair a veil over her face, with Fred spread on top of her chest, a black-and-white comma. On the coffee table next to her sits a glowing orange plate with a pale green cupcake wrapper and dark chocolate crumbs. Those last years of Amy's life, Jane worried that she'd find Amy had stopped breathing. That was indeed how she had found her.

Jane snaps photos of Eve and Byron in the backyard with Ginger Rogers. She'll ask Vihaan to help her print them out later, and she'll add them to the empty pages of the last photo album.

Byron and Eve join the housemates for dinner that they help Jane make, flatbread with ricotta and marinated artichoke hearts, Caesar salad. After dinner, they watch Pearl and Doris play chess, while again Byron holds Jane's hands. The handholding and the cold water this morning have proven therapeutic. Jane remembers hearing about a group of Cambodians who had gone blind after witnessing the genocide and how there'd been nothing wrong with their eyes. They'd just seen too much. In Jane's case, she's had too much to handle. It feels as if Byron's hands are pulling out and detangling Jane's knotted electric currents of trouble, unraveling them so the power can stop shocking her and instead start flowing through her, out of her fingertips.

Jane, her visitors, and Barry walk around the sculpture park. They stand under *Looking Up,* a stainless steel man who's taller than the nearby palm trees and who's indeed peering up at the striated sky. Jane uses her hand as a visor, and Byron does the same.

Around the park are benches, and they stop to sit. Two peacocks come strutting down the trail, seemingly conversing with each other through their meows.

"What do you think their relationship is?" Barry says.

Jane replies, "Either they're a couple, or they knew each other in 'Nam."

In the lake skirting the park are hundreds of dormant lily pads, a freckled brown. Jane has visited in the spring and fall when they were in full bloom. She exhales, and her breath makes a cloud, the air tasting metallic as if she were licking the sculpture of the cloud-gazer.

After Byron and Eve drive off on their journey, Jane feels fatigued, as if she has arrived home after a trip herself. In the yard, Ginger is playing with a thread from Jane's unraveled sweater, and the rest of the sweater is nowhere to be seen, maybe scattered in the grasses and the branches or, better, padding a nest.

In the weeks after the visit, Jane's tremor subsides. Whether the tremor will return or not, she enjoys the reprieve.

Chapter 12: Waltz

THEY LEAF THROUGH their Playbills, and Pearl strokes the velvety cover of her seat. Pearl, Doris, and Vihaan are Barry's guests at the performance. Their seats are front and center, and Pearl recalls sitting close to the stage at a standup comedian's performance. As he whipped around to face stage left, a mist of perspiration flew off him, a drop of which landed on Pearl's lap.

On Mondays, the four housemates gather around to watch a dance competition show called *Dance, Yes You Can!* and one week the show featured a guest spot by a physically integrated dance troupe of people in wheelchairs and people who aren't. They're touring and appearing tonight at the university's performing center. The lights dim, and the stage lights up with splashes of magenta and apricot.

If you can fall elegantly, that's what one of the men in a wheelchair does from his chair, and he pulls himself across the stage by his powerful arms as if the stage were water and he is doing the breaststroke. Another man does the same at the opposite end of the stage, and the men pass each other center stage.

A woman stands behind the chair of another woman and tips her back, to the gasp of the audience, raises her, tips her, raises her, the movement like the inhalation and exhalation of an accordion's bellows.

Eight people in wheelchairs pair up to form petals of a flower radiating out from a man pirouetting in the center. The dancers in chairs pulse inward and outward, left and right, glowing in the dimmed lights, a Busby Berkeley allusion.

Behind a dancer in a chair, two other dancers stand and interweave their arms with his so he appears to have six arms, fingers snapping to the Bollywood music. Pearl thinks of the many arms in her household, how they take turns spinning in the domestic clockwork.

She looks at the side of Barry's face, a vein by his broad forehead a pale blue. On Pearl's other side is Doris whom she has succeeded in letting go, not without pain but by needing to believe that Doris and all of her housemates have enough love to go around. Doris is wearing a silk scarf that looks like a rainbow chrysalis around her long neck.

When the local pool reopens in a couple of months, Pearl wants to go and see what it's like to swim with simply her arms to pull her through the water, letting her legs be buoyed by the water but not using them to propel forward.

At work, Pearl smells Ruby before she sees her.

Ruby greets her with a pat on the arm. "I wanted to tell you, Pearl, that I had to move. The police were cracking down on the encampment. We found another place to sleep, for now."

"I was worried about you," Pearl says.

"I'm sorry."

Pearl nods. Later, she finds Ruby back in her chair, slouched and reading an old *Gourmet* magazine. Pearl says, "I'm leaving work soon. Would you like to go for ice cream?"

"Delighted."

Ruby insists on treating Pearl, paying with quarters and nickels. As before, they get a wide berth, a man in line behind them glaring at them. When they sit at the table, the man takes an adjacent table, spreading his arms and legs to claim his space. He mutters under his breath until his voice starts getting louder, cranking up the volume.

He leaps up from his seat and looms over Ruby. "Where'd you get that money from?"

Ruby winces and scoots away as far as she can on the booth bench.

Pearl asks, "What's your issue?"

The man ignores her. "Where'd you get that money?"

Ruby says, "I was given it."

"Well, I'm one of the people who gave it to you." He's yelling now. "My tax dollars. Not to be used on fancy ice cream. You didn't earn it."

"Stop it. Right now," Pearl says to the man in the no-nonsense voice she uses at the library if a kid is mauling a book. She gives several dismissive nods.

One of the ice cream servers has come out from behind the counter and says, "Sir, I'm going to have to ask you to keep your voice down."

The man throws his half-eaten cone at Ruby, hitting the side of her head, and storms out.

The server gets a cup of water and some napkins with which Ruby tries to dab off the ice cream as she wears a grim smile, her eyes distant. The ice cream has melted into the top of Ruby's sweater and is dripping down.

Pearl fishes a comb from her purse and gives it to Ruby. "Don't know if this will help. I'm going to see if the shower's available."

"I'd appreciate that."

She calls Doris. The others in the background come to a consensus that it's fine for Ruby to come over.

Ruby is sniffling and rubbing her damp hair as they walk back to West House. Pearl hands her a Kleenex and keeps looking over her shoulder to make sure the harasser isn't following them. She thinks of how vulnerable Ruby is sleeping out in the open, nowhere to hide.

At the house, Pearl finds clean clothes that she doesn't mind giving away, and while Ruby is in the shower, Pearl starts the laundry with Ruby's few garments. Barry has prepared BLTs for Pearl and Ruby, and they eat them while the other housemates join them at the table and pass around a couple of bottles of seltzer. Pearl sees Ruby eyeing the flat half of Ellen's shirt; Ellen catches her too and nods. Ruby pats her heart.

On a Monday night, they're watching their dance show. All the dancers are young and spry, capable of bouncing back, their feet like springs. Dressed in identical filmy black-and-white suits, a couple waltzes. Doris pulls Vihaan up from the couch and attempts to lead him in a waltz; he follows clumsily, both of them laughing. Barry claps along, then extends a hand to Pearl, and they galumph around the living room too.

At the end of the dance, they plop back into their seats, Pearl catching her breath. It's much easier just to sit and watch. Her bones feel creaky, hamstrings tight as a drum.

At the library, Pearl is doing story time when she hears a man shouting. She shuts the door to the story room and ventures out to see what's happening.

The man has backed Ruby into a shelf of books. It's the man from the ice cream shop, his eyes slits, his chest heaving. "You're stealing from me!" he shouts. "You're a fucking leech. And you smell like shit." His hands are in fists a few inches from Ruby's face. "I could crush you."

Pearl dials 911 and whispers her report. Before the police arrive, the man yanks armloads of books from the shelves and kicks them around the floor while Ruby crouches on the ground, shielding her face.

At the sound of a siren, the man runs out of the library, and the checkout librarian catches his license plate number.

The story time kids' caretakers are ushering them out of the room, holding the smaller kids in their arms and keeping their hands on the older kids' shoulders. Pearl hovers around Ruby, trying to comfort her.

"How can I help?" Pearl says.

"Can you take me to the downtown branch? I'd feel safer there, I think."

After Pearl and the others give the police a report, the branch manager grants Pearl the rest of the day off.

Barry drives over in the Odyssey, and the three of them head to the downtown branch. Ruby sits tense in the front passenger seat, her arm stiff but hanging out the open window, her eyes closed. Pearl sits in the back, and with her feet, she stirs the dead leaves on the floor mat. They pull up to the unloading spot at the library. When Barry tries to give Ruby a wad of cash, she refuses at first, but he persuades her to take it, and she tucks it into her shoe.

Pearl moves to the passenger seat for the ride home. "I thought he was going to hit her," she says. "I thought of throwing a book at him. I could see it sailing through the air and slicing his head, as if it were a knife. Violence begets violence. But after calling 911, I was frozen."

Barry grasps her hand. "That must have been so scary," he says.

"Especially for poor Ruby." Pearl nods and nods. She remembers Vihaan with his homemade tennis ball, talking about bullies, as he stood next to the sinkhole, trying to vanquish the memories.

Back at home, Pearl stands by the sink, clutching her midnight blue mug, drinking cup after cup of water until her stomach says no. She runs her finger over a chip on the mug's lip, and the mug slips out of her hand, cracking into many pieces on the floor. As she sweeps up the pieces, she chastises herself for not being more careful with something so breakable.

Pearl calls the desk at the central branch, and the librarian is willing to look for Ruby in the section where Pearl had seen her a while back. The librarian takes Ruby to the phone.

"It's Pearl. Just seeing how you are."

"Okay enough, thank you."

"Want to come for a shower Monday night?"

"What's today?"

"Friday."

They arrange a pickup.

On Monday evening, after Ruby showers, she joins the group of them watching the dance show in the living room. The young dancers are wearing old-people wigs and makeup. They morph from doing the Charleston with a faux and anachronistic New York skyline in the background to a strutting disco hustle under a mirror ball that descends from the ceiling.

Ruby is leaning forward, her chin in her hands, and Pearl pictures a younger Ruby in a philosophy class a few rows away from Barry. Ruby laughs at the dance show judges' snarky assessments.

After the show, Pearl goes to get Ruby's clothes from the dryer. They warm her hands like the fluffy gloves Pearl used to wear in the Michigan winter. She hands the clothes to Ruby, hoping there's enough warmth left to comfort her too.

When Pearl asks, Ruby is indeed interested in watching a video of the dancers in wheelchairs swirling around the dancers standing up. "Resilient," says Ruby.

The pool is open, and Pearl is swimming laps in a lane next to Doris. She lets her legs dangle, resists using them, and her arms do indeed pull her along. The sun dapples the water here and there, creating sliding diamonds. Under the water, it sounds like wind chimes. For this hour, Pearl has nothing to worry about.

After supper, they clear the dining table completely and have an art night, with Ellen and Tomás supplying the materials. Pearl draws a beached dead seabird, its stomach cut open and filled with tufts of plastic. She paints a duck coated in black oil. She sketches a turtle choked by a six-pack ring. Afterward, she puts her images in the shredder, enjoying the power to destroy them.

Chapter 13:
Boundless and Fleeting

"Marjoram," Vihaan says.

Doris says, "Peoria."

"Winnebago."

"For a male or a female?"

"Unisex. Also Tricot."

"Okay, good night."

The housemates chipped in for Vihaan's and Doris's June birthdays and gifted them a weekend at a cottage in the Hill Country. This is the first time they've been able to sleep together in the same bed, and Vihaan has learned that Doris snores. He wrestles with whether to wake her. She wanted to see the sun rise, and it's almost time. They can rest later. He first whispers and taps her shoulder, says her name more loudly, and then she says his. As she stretches, he admires her arms.

He rises to brush his teeth and finds a scorpion is in the sink. He can't tell if it's alive because it's still, as if posing for a picture. In the unfamiliar kitchen, he rummages around until he finds a broom and dustpan. He feels squeamish but manages to get the scorpion in the dustpan. It wriggles, obeying its nature. He hastens out the back door, afraid it will crawl up his arm, and throws it over the fence into a field.

He reports back to Doris, who's standing by the brewing coffee, and they agree that they need to wear shoes and keep their eyes open. He thinks about how he's been delving into this connection with Doris with the emotional equivalent of bare feet and carefree eyes. He wants it to stay that way.

They watch the sun rise from the porch swing and go ambling, sidestepping mounds of fire ants here and there. They hover over one mound, trying to count the ants, then give up. Their leisure today seems both boundless and fleeting. In the distance, the hills of ash juniper and limestone are studded with new luxurious homes.

After savoring breakfast muffins and orange juice left by the cottage proprietors, they return to bed. As he drifts off, Vihaan remembers when his parents were quite old, they would catnap the day away and stay up watching late shows and Turner Classics at night. Their retirement had allowed them to return to their night owl natures, the way they were before they forced themselves in their work and family life to be early birds. By their contortions, they gave Vihaan and his brothers their version of the American Dream—except they'd saddled the three sons with names their teachers and classmates had trouble pronouncing. Still, they wouldn't have blended into their town even if they were called Tom, Dick, and Harry.

It's difficult, in a good way, to sleep with Doris pressed into him. He sees in his mind's eye the images Pearl did of ravaged sea creatures. He washes the oily duck and sets it back afloat. With a pang, he realizes he will never see a coral reef, except in pictures. A highlight of his career was playing at the Australian Open, but his coach had insisted that Vihaan couldn't risk the possibility of injury if he did anything outside the box, like going to see a coral reef. Somehow, later, there never seemed to be time or money for international travel.

On art night, he'd created an abstract that, unbeknownst to the others, was a magnified version of Doris's variegated hair, the strands glossy with tiny barbs to give them dimension. Back when his son, Will, was young, one of their favorite exhibits at the children's museum was the one in which they had to guess what an extreme close-up depicted. The camera would pan out farther and farther until one of the family was able to guess the object. Will was so good at abstractions. Maybe Vihaan needs to understand more what Will does for a living. That prospect eases him into sleep.

She wakes him by brushing her fingers through his hair. She's wearing a camisole and nothing else. There's the sex question. His attraction is there, a constant, but his body is slow to burn, flickering on and off. She has told him she feels the same. Sexually, they wander together, stopping to lean against a tree, only occasionally reaching a clearing, a destination.

They move to the back of the cottage, lying in a double hammock from which they can see the sun set. In a fantasy world, Vihaan would live in a place like this, designed to allow the easy viewings of sunrise and sunset. Isn't it enough to have the opportunity today? Maybe he wouldn't appreciate the views so much if they were readily available—yes, he would. If he could appreciate thwacking a ball for the kazillionth time, he could always admire the sky's fires. Today, he sees what's coloring the sky while picturing random strangers watching the sun set from their perches urban, rural, nearby, and as far away as they can be and still be on Earth.

"Wonders never cease," Doris whispers. "By the way, a girl could be named Giardia."

"First and middle names: Naval Jelly," he responds.

When they're back inside, Vihaan sees that his brother, Dev, from New York has called four times in the span of an hour. No message. For decades now, they've spoken every third Sunday, and this is a mere six days from when they last spoke. Vihaan had been half-hoping for no cell signal out in the country. He clenches his teeth. "Do you mind if I call Dev?" Their cocoon, poked. It has to be bad news, he tells Doris. Except when their children were born, they've never interrupted their schedule for good news.

Doris says, "Of course, you should call him back. If you want to."

"Please sit next to me." Just six months ago, he wouldn't have asked anyone to be in the room.

Dev answers and says, "Sanjay left us." Their other brother.

Vihaan is and isn't surprised. "Do you mean he died?" he asks. Doris squeezes his hand.

"You know what I mean. Why are you quibbling?"

"Pills? Gun?"

"He wouldn't have a gun. He hasn't changed that much."

"Who found him?"

"Who do you think?"

"You could have called me right away."

"I called 911, and I'm waiting for them. Anaya's on her way." Dev's wife.

"Oh, shit." Vihaan holds his face with his free hand, swallows, and says, "FaceTime me."

Doris whispers, "Are you sure?"

"It will stick with you," Dev says. "I should have just called you later."

"Let me. Doris is here." Dev had met Doris back at the college co-op when he'd breezed through town. Dev had been well off enough to treat a couple of Vihaan's friends to a meal outside the co-op. That seemed a couple of lifetimes ago.

Dev shows Vihaan the postage-stamp apartment, the stacks of papers and magazines, *New York Times*, *Washington Post*, and

The Economist. He shows him the rug that might have been beige fifty years ago. Sanjay would allow no one to help him clean up.

Dev shows him the pristine section of the one wall that Sanjay allowed to be repainted, on which his various teaching accolades were framed. He'd been fired for talking too much about politics in the journalism classes he taught. Sanjay had insisted, "Someone has to speak up." He had master's degrees in journalism, history, and political science. He couldn't stand that the current emperor in chief had no clothes.

"Just show me Sanjay," Vihaan says.

"The fucking miracles of modern technology," Dev says. "Why don't you wait until he's cleaned up?"

"You called me for a reason right now. I love you." They never say that to each other.

Sanjay is twisted, his face with its ragged beard, his neck, his leg, the sheet bunched around his bare gray ankle.

Dev says, "The note on his table says, 'Always too much. Never enough. Burden. Next time. Better me.'"

"What the hell?"

"I wouldn't have been surprised," Dev says, "if he'd hurt someone else." Brooding Sanjay had bubbled with anger.

"If he was going to take himself out, maybe it wouldn't have been so bad if he took Brett Kavanaugh with him."

"Or Mitch McConnell. Can I see him again?"

Dev sweeps the camera across Sanjay's stillness. He picks up a magazine, ruffles its pages, and a few silverfish fall out.

"Let's look in his fridge," Dev says, as if that would somehow be more revealing than a note. In the fridge are a couple of shriveled clementines, a pitcher with water and lots of fingerprints on its side, a jar of mango chutney. "Best before 8/1/13." Over six years ago. The fridge contents don't look so different from Vihaan's after Rose died and Vihaan had little appetite.

If Vihaan were there, he would have untwisted Sanjay from the sheet, as if somehow Sanjay would be more comfortable with a smooth sheet. He would look at Sanjay's body to find more clues, though there's nothing that Sanjay's body could say to reassure Vihaan.

Dev will hire someone to get rid of Sanjay's worn possessions. Neither of them can imagine wanting anything from the apartment. Dev says a rushed goodbye when someone rings the doorbell.

Vihaan feels dizzy, so he lies in bed, his head on Doris's chest, rising, falling. "I didn't see him the last time I was in New York," he says. "That was for the reunion at Barry's."

"You didn't know."

"Every time I saw him, he still talked about the marriage he had in his twenties and how she left him because he wouldn't get treatment for his depression. He said he wouldn't be able to find a therapist or doctor who was as smart as he was. Rose once said about him that he was 'terminally unique.'"

It seems petty now, but he'd also been irritated with Sanjay about how when Dev offered to pay for him to attend Rose's memorial, Sanjay turned down the offer. He hadn't followed up with Vihaan to see how he was doing with the loss of Rose, though Vihaan would have been shocked if he had.

If he keeps thinking about how Sanjay disappointed him, embarrassed him with his rants when they would meet up in the city, Sanjay talking with a mouthful of food, pushing more food onto his fork with his hand, if Vihaan keeps piling up these alienating moments, then he can avoid thinking about how much Sanjay must have suffered.

"I couldn't help him," Vihaan says.

"I know," Doris replies.

He tells Doris about Sanjay's paper route to save up for a telescope, Sanjay's endless letters to the editor, Sanjay's marathon sessions at the Metropolitan Museum of Art. Sanjay's rashes, his wolfish smile, his love of violet candies that smelled like soap.

Later, Doris soothes him to sleep with a recitation of names; she remembers the ones from before as if she'd been asked to memorize them for a cognitive test. She adds, "Citric, teak, saltpeter, tissue." The names of children they'll never have.

Chapter 14: The Art of Silence

DORIS ASKS VIHAAN if she can sleep in his bed while he's gone to New York for the memorial, and he has no problem with that. The white in the room glows in the gray darkness, a nightlight of sorts. The sheets are as soft as flannel.

She'll be subbing at a nearby high school today, and Barry drops her off there. After smoothing her skirt, she enters the building, greeting the security guards who search her purse and lunch bag.

She's asked the class to write a sequel chapter to *The Great Gatsby*, and they're relatively quiet, heads bowed over their laptops, a foot tapping here and a tic-like throat clearing there, when a voice comes over the loudspeaker.

"Attention, all students and staff. A full lockdown is now in effect. Attention. Attention."

She's been trained, as have the students. She locks the door while a student closes the classroom curtains, a puff of dust floating up from the fabric's folds. They pass around the basket of phones, and the students silence them. They push desks to block the doorway, as if an active shooter would need to spring over the tangle of desks to do them harm. A cluster of young women is huddling in the "safe" corner, heads together, arms around each other. Doris stands near them and feels sad for the young men making themselves as small as possible individually One of them is tugging on his patchy goatee, the skin underneath growing red.

If someone enters the classroom, she will throw herself to the front, take a bullet. She's had a full life, had her share, unlike these unfortunates. Pushing the air in front of her, she spreads her arms against an invisible enemy, her body a rope of resistance.

A siren sounds in the distance but peters out.

She pictures the sinkhole on her cul-de-sac sucking through the illusion of the ordinary to reveal the turmoil that's been building, growing in fits and starts until it gathers momentum and can't be stopped.

She'd been wanting to cut back on the substitute teaching but has been afraid of what that would mean financially.

One young person seems to be choking back vomit and then sinks to the floor and goes into child's pose, a relaxing yoga position usually done at the end of a session.

Doris recalls reading about Marcel Marceau, the famous French pantomimist, and how he first mimed to quiet the Jewish children during World War II as he helped them escape to neutral Switzerland. She is thirsty, and she mimes pouring herself a drink of water from a pitcher. A young man notices and holds out an invisible cup into which she pours another glass of water.

A gender-bending individual with a lavender ponytail, crouched and leaning against a wall, pretends to be in a tight box, pushing in vain with hands and feet to get out of it.

Soundlessly, another person laughs with her whole body, wiping away real tears.

A young woman lifts an imaginary conductor's baton, and soon, as the conductor dips at the knees and rises, jabbing and slicing the air, the students are playing an invisible piccolo, a violin, a cello, a sax. Is that a triangle? She wonders what music the students have playing in their heads. Probably tunes she's never heard. She wishes that instead of having them write a new chapter of *The Great Gatsby*, she'd suggested that they each share from their phones a song they love. There had never been enough time to hear from each student at any length or depth.

From the direction of the hall comes the sound of shoes slapping the floor, one pair, two, three, too hard to distinguish. The students curl up on themselves as if trying not to breathe in tear gas; some squeeze their eyes shut.

Doris's hands start to shake with anger that someone's presuming to rob them of their freedom, the freedom to ignore the possibility of death. She wants to scream, hears her voice inside her head shrieking the command, "Peace!"

Last time she subbed at the school, the hubbub had been about a raccoon that had fallen through a ceiling tile and was scrambling around the desks. A rabid raccoon, a swarm of locusts, a pack of wolves, just no guns, please.

What she might never see again: Vihaan's five-o'clock shadow, dandelion fluff floating, Pearl's chin moving up and down, her red Chuck Taylors, Ellen and Tomás shoulder to shoulder, a Torrey pine, Barry cleaning a cast-iron pan with baking soda, the smudges of dancers' footprints on the rec center linoleum, Jane petting Ginger, a mimosa in bloom, David returning Vihaan's serve.

She might never pee again or have another bite of toast. She's feeling dizzy, and the students dissolve into circles, chevrons, triangles, then snap back together into breathing, sweating, crying fellow humans.

She might not believe it when a voice comes over the loudspeaker. "Attention. Lockdown order now lifted. Suspects apprehended." Maybe whoever made the announcement is conning them, casting out a seductive illusion of safety. No, she doesn't believe it, even when the assistant principal opens the door and says, "We're okay." Speak for yourself.

The students file out of the classroom one by one, shaking her hand or hugging her as they pass, as if they were crossing the stage at a grim graduation. The student to whom she'd given the invisible cup of water holds one out to her.

Marcel Marceau called miming "the art of silence."

Doris collapses onto Barry when he arrives to pick her up. The school parking lot looks abnormally normal, an orderly line of cars exiting. Barry has no clue what had gone on at the school, and she weeps as she tells him the story.

Back at home, the housemates crush her in their hugs. She retires to Vihaan's room and stares at the ceiling as if looking at the night sky, searching in vain for peace.

Chapter 15: Invisible

ON THE CHECKOUT line at Nature's Share, Ellen and Tomás have a basket full of toilet paper, paper towels, soaps, dried mangoes and peaches, and cashews. Behind them, a woman stands too close, using a compostable spork to scoop and swallow straight from a tub of freshly ground peanut butter. Tomás is tempted to tell the woman that he has a peanut allergy.

"I don't know what the big deal is," the woman says. "Lot of fuss about a little virus. The flu kills ..." Her hot breath wafts toward them.

Ellen scoots farther away from the woman. She's told Tomás that he's too polite, always responding to whomever, as if he were running for political office. "But it's part of why I love you," she'd said.

At home, Barry is reading the paper, scouring the news for more information about the virus. He remembers back in the '80s when the press started noticing a "gay cancer." He sighs and finds Jane, who commiserates about this new terror, and they vow to wash their hands more often. They take off on a spot-the-bluebonnets walk, and Jane asks, "Does our sinkhole look a little crusty?"

The repair had made the street black and silky at first, but now abrasion has rendered it rougher, grayer. "I feel crusty," Barry says, wiping a bit of sleep from the corner of his eye. Through the grapevine, he's heard that the Quilted Pig is closing for the week, with New York shutting down in general for a little while to give the virus a chance to run its course.

Jane gazes at the lilac blossoms of the misnomered redbud trees.

Vihaan can't keep up with David on the court today. Since Sanjay died, Vihaan has felt as if he were trudging through sludge, his legs and arms heavy and threatening to crumple when he tries to move at his usual speed. He finds himself muttering, "You're messed up," though he doesn't know if he's talking to himself or to his brother or to the world at large. He doesn't understand how he can miss Sanjay when, for so many years, he dreaded seeing him or talking with him. He misses the Sanjay of childhood, the one who could laugh at himself, who had patience with Vihaan as he struggled through high school math. Vihaan's new sneakers are biting his skin, giving him blisters, and he has to hobble home from the court. He wants to throw out the new shoes; they're the same brand, size, style as the old ones but inflexible, nonetheless. In his bedroom, he stuffs the new sneakers into the wastebasket, then withdraws them. He inserts a large Progresso soup can into each shoe, trying to have faith that, with a stretch, these sneakers will become more comfortable. He wants to grow his patience.

Doris and Pearl are baking dulce de leche cookies. Doris still feels shaken by the school lockdown of course; it's a low rumble on her radar. Even though no one was wounded, Doris stays aware in a prickly way of how the high school with its earnest pursuits and seeming good will could have turned into a shooting gallery.

Pearl says, "I feel the same way about when the guy terrorized Ruby at the library. Public, sacred space. Poof!" She's nibbling on a teaspoonful of raw cookie batter, despite warnings about such behavior.

"And now we have an invisible threat." Doris holds her breath and waves her hand through the air as if she could grasp something microscopic and rub it into oblivion between her fingers. "If you get food poisoning from that cookie dough, it's not a good time to go to the hospital."

"Oh, there aren't cases here in town, are there?"

"Surely there must be."

At dinner, Vihaan avoids scratching the blisters that now itch. He concentrates instead on studying Doris's eyebrows, the arches that easily make her appear surprised. She sees him watching her and smiles, a balm.

"To your health," says Ellen, raising a glass and tipping it toward each of them.

"And yours," says Tomás, dropping a kiss on the top of her head.

"So, what are we going to do about this virus?" asks Barry.

"Wait, look!" says Jane, as if she has found an antidote. She points to the male and female cardinal pair perching on the fence.

Tomás appreciates the brightness in the male's red feathers and the subtlety of the female's red and creamy brown. A mourning dove is calling from nearby.

After dinner, they watch a video of a treatment center in China where the COVID patients dance to strengthen their lungs. Any patients who don't have the strength to dance are funneled to more intensive care.

Barry cues up James Brown, and soon they're the ones dancing. Pearl sings along, "'I feel good. Like I knew that I would,'" as she pumps her fists in the air.

Jane's shaking her hips and rubbing her hands. She finds that if she massages her hands for a few minutes daily, the tremors stay subterranean. She can still feel a current now and then, a mild shock, but her hands remain steady.

No one has answered Barry's question about what they'll do about the virus because there is no answer except vigilance, staying informed.

Pearl goes back to the table for another dulce de leche cookie because who knows how long she has to live? It's always a balancing act between instant gratification versus delay. At least, she can try to savor the cookie, letting it melt in her mouth, the dough turning to sweet sand, the caramel sticky warm.

Vihaan is reeling Doris out, then pulling her back in, dipping her. "Don't hurt yourself," she says, taking a deep breath. "Or me."

Barry thinks about how he needs to talk to the housemates about Cliff and David. He doesn't want to stop seeing them, particularly Cliff, but maybe that'd be wise, fair. He'd be fine with restricting Ruby's visits because she seems to pose more of a risk to the household than David or Cliff, who both have the luxuries of solitude and good hygiene. He has to admit to himself that he still has trouble with the way Ruby smells, has yet to become nose-blind.

He feels shitty closing the door on the person his mother or father might have become had he and his siblings been unable to help out financially. Still, maybe he's doing enough being a safety net for his housemates and contributing cold, hard virtual cash to the community. He swallows his pangs of conscience with the swirls of red wine at the bottom of his nightly glass.

Ellen is considering Cliff. She's been pleased to see someone who so overtly delights in Barry. Because she feels obliged to refrain from the surplus of affection she has for Barry, it's satisfying to see him receive an abundance from a kind and bright source. She'd watched the two of them ice skating last week, arm in arm and then holding gloved hands as Cliff skated backwards. She feels too brittle to try skating, but she can get a vicarious thrill by watching them. She wonders what Barry feels watching her and

Tomás. Barry's dancing now, the Robot, his silver-gray shirt appropriate for a metal creature. At a West House New Year's Eve dance, back during college, Barry had garnered their admiration by doing the splits and somersaults. Tomás, who drank a bunch in those days, had passed out and missed the show.

Vihaan and Doris fall onto the couch together, their arms intertwined. He'd forgotten his blisters, and now they throb again.

Pearl plops down on the other end of the couch, fanning herself with one hand. When she does a long exhale, she sounds like a horse; she tries to create the sound again but fails.

Tomás fills his lungs and holds his breath as if he were underwater. He entitled one of his old paintings *Capacious,* and that's what he wants to be. The painting had featured an abstract pair of brown lungs floating in a pellucid stream.

Neighbor David is at the door. "Should we let him in, or are we quarantining?" Jane asks. She feels as if everyone's a suspect now.

"I just saw him for tennis this afternoon," says Vihaan. He tries to think of a polite way to ask David if he'd been swapping spit with anyone since then. He doubts it.

"Quick show of hands," Barry says. The vote to open the door is a unanimous yes. Pearl waves David into a chair in the living room and sets a plate of cookies in front of him.

"I just wanted to see how you're all faring with the news," David says.

"I'm already sick of it," says Ellen.

They play Trivial Pursuit because everyone's ready for trivia and no one's ready to say goodnight anytime soon. It's after midnight when David leaves. The one other time they'd all stayed up this late in this new incarnation of West House had been for New Year's.

After David is gone, the only lights shining are in their bed rooms and by the sinks in the bathroom and kitchen, where they all line up to wash hands, each singing "Happy Birthday," the recommended accompaniment when trying to banish germs.

Chapter 16: No, No, Yes, and No

ELLEN REMINDS TOMÁS of all the noes they and their roommates are facing. "No folk dancing."

"Poor Doris. I did enjoy that one time I went with her."

"I thought we might invite ourselves along sometime. Well, how long can this virus last anyhow?" They are lying in bed, Ellen in her crimson robe, Tomás in peacock blue boxer briefs. Ellen is absentmindedly smoothing the flat part of her chest.

"No library for Pearl," Ellen says. "No running into Ruby."

"Not good." Ellen and Tomás have also been enjoying their putters around the Ann Richards library branch, where they each choose one book for themselves and one they'll both read.

"I think Cliff and Barry are going to go through ice skating withdrawal."

"Now I can't even watch them," Ellen says.

"I know you like to watch," he says.

She kisses the back of his hand. "No tennis for Vihaan. He's going to be crabby."

"Ah, but he has Doris now. Plus he's got the lungs and heart of a forty-year-old."

"No substitute teaching in person for Doris. We were hoping she'd quit for good anyway."

"No big-screen movies."

"We were trying to conserve anyway."

"It's not that we were going and splurging there very often. But it's that we can't."

"Yeah, the forbidden fruit, like how I never wanted raw fish as much as I did when I was pregnant."

No museums, no getaways (though Barry is the only one still in a position to afford them). No to having over Ruby, whom Pearl hasn't run into lately anyway.

Yes walks, yes sitting in the yard, yes complaints, yes worries, yes obsessions, yes anxiety dreams, yes discussion then dismissal of getting a bidet. Yes to letting David and Cliff into the group after discussing with them who would be in their social groups (David's ex, and Cliff claimed he was satisfied with just Barry and company). Tomás reminds Ellen of all these yesses, some of them most unwelcome, she notes.

"No to making new friends," Ellen says. "Yes to strengthening ties with old friends."

"No to in-person volunteer work. Yes to more artwork." He's begun creating half-inch spiky coronavirus balls out of duct tape strips of various colors. Ellen is fashioning them into earrings and pendants. "Admit it. You don't want to make new friends anyhow."

"It's been a while," she says. "In fact, I can't remember the last friend I made. If I were my best self, I would have interest in new friends." After her old friend died of breast cancer, she made no new friends.

"We have enough. David and Cliff are kind of new friends."

"Kind of."

"Yes to unfathomable numbers contracting the virus. No to anyone we know contracting it yet."

"We don't know whether we know anyone."

They read obituaries to honor the dead, but they can't keep up. Ellen memorizes the names of someone's children—Nathan, Natalia, Natasha—and she hears the names like a chant as she tries to fall asleep. She reads a family obituary: two parents, an uncle, two sisters, and a brother; she tries to imprint their names and succeeds for a day, but they vanish soon thereafter. When she thinks of the West House family pierced by illness, she feels the start of a panic attack.

"You're being morbid," Tomás comments when he sees Ellen's sketchbook of strangers from the obits.

"I find it soothing," she says. "What's wrong with memorializing people?"

"Strangers."

"I don't know how else to behave that seems vaguely constructive."

"Fair enough."

She doesn't tell him that she's considering getting on strangers' online memorial accounts and writing that, though she didn't know them, she was touched by the obituary. She could also include a thumbnail portrait. Or maybe it isn't her damn business and she needs to butt out.

"I don't need your approval," she says.

"Ouch," Tomás says.

Creeping out of dormancy comes Tomás's obsession with his eyesight and with the possible lack of early warning signs. Look at how Trump and his cronies hid the severity of the virus, and now that's killing thousands. He doesn't want to be a hypochondriac, but are objects more hazy? Now he definitely can't go nag the eye doctor because her office will be a place not to get better but to potentially pick up something deadly. His eyes can wait.

He remembers how he used to shut off his ruminating mind many years ago, before Ellen begged him to stop. Maybe it's safe to take just a sip, a few sips, of a sour, crisp beer, the fizz disintegrating the pebbles of obsession that have started keeping him awake at night again. He was able to stop drinking before, and this will be for just one evening.

"I'm ready for a beer," says Tomás to Ellen as he pours one.
"Are you sure?" Ellen holds up a stop-sign hand.
"Yes."
"Please think it over some more."

He wants to tell her to trust him but doesn't know if he can trust himself. He's already tired of the noes and allows himself this yes. The drink works. Now what?

Chapter 17: How Alone

Vihaan is winded. A walk to the empty tennis court feels all uphill, though it isn't, and fevered, though the breeze is crisp. His breath is shallow and shaky, and his thirst for the reassuring beverage of normal wellness is unquenchable, frightening. After he tests positive, he quarantines at Cliff's Airbnb since it's empty after the city cancels its usual spring music festival.

The roommates test negative. Doris calls Vihaan's clients whom he hasn't seen in a couple of weeks, but still … No one reports illness.

The pain Vihaan had in his knee last year seems to have spread throughout his body, a cattle prod here and there just as he's about to drift off. He can't help wincing in preparation for the next shock. He is a tight fetal ball warding off blows.

Three times a day he finds a meal on a foil-covered sturdy paper plate outside his door. It looks like the handiwork of Barry, who knows even more than Doris what Vihaan might like to eat or might stomach—pancakes, silky chicken salad, a Chinese-style rice porridge. Still, the food won't stay down or in.

All his exercise, his young heart, was supposed to ward this off. He can't imagine when he'll be ready to die, but it's certainly not now. The doctor who's monitoring his symptoms by phone and by Vihaan's pulse oximeter reports assures him that he can stay away from the hospital. "You need time," the doctor says.

Vihaan gets a moment's reassurance from this prognosis, but what if the doctor's wrong?

The roommates want him to rest without interruption but are also afraid of silences from him. They, mostly Doris, call twice a day.

"Why you?" she asks him.

Today he's able to respond, "Why not me?"

His temperature is 103, and he shivers. When he catches himself holding his breath, he lets it whoosh out. He imagines he's dangling from the ceiling like a figure in a lackluster Chagall. He wipes what feels like ash from the corners of his eyes. What did he learn by being laid up on the couch all those months ago? What he knows today: What was bad then was a hell of a lot less scary than what he's going through now. When he'd lay still back then at the house, when'd he felt cracked open, his unexpected romance with Doris had evolved.

Now his daydream vision of a cracked-open peaceful walnut morphs into a cracked, shredded, and angry lobster claw, and he bends over the toilet with dry heaves. There is nothing redeeming about this illness.

It has been a day. It has been a month. It has been ten years. He must be breathing because he wakes up alive, mouth gluey, fingers flimsy and unbending as popsicle sticks. Hauling himself to the bathroom feels as if he's walking on ground glass.

His son, Will, can't come visit, of course, but calls every day. Vihaan hasn't seen Will's face in three dimensions since four years ago when they took the trip to New York that Rose had asked them to take. She knew Will liked Broadway musicals and Vihaan liked the Metropolitan Museum, and she'd wanted them drawn together to fill the space she left. "Maybe it could be a yearly thing," she'd mused, as if she were a glassblower spinning the time, money, and inclination they'd yet to have.

"I'm worried about you, Dad," says Will.

"I understand. I am too." Vihaan wants to make promises of better times, but he can't find the words for a genuine reassurance.

The sirens seem constant, and Vihaan imagines himself whirling in a colossal blender full of ambulances. He will ask for earplugs. In the meantime, he sings silently to himself: "Help" by the Beatles and "This Land Is Your Land" by Woody Guthrie.

He stops using artificial light because it feels painful, as if it's a weight he has to carry. When it's dark, he sleeps. He discovers that slumber has many more gradations than he could detect when he was well.

The food now has no taste or scent, and he simply eats to fill the tank. If he could just breathe more deeply, he wouldn't be weeping about the apple that's like cardboard. The wet of the tears is a balm on his aching face. He says aloud, "You are loved." Then he chants "You love" over and over to reassure himself, to blur the fear that he will not survive this.

He can't get comfortable in bed one night, feeling as if he's continually near to falling off the mattress, so he gets as low as he can, the bare floor, its immovability, its lack of give somehow soothing, he in starfish position. The floors are bamboo, and he wants to absorb bamboo's tendency to proliferate, to regenerate. Now he can return to the mattress and let it cradle him in its contrasting softness.

Vihaan has mostly isolated in the bedroom, as far away from the front door as possible, as if that will keep his germs more contained. Today, he stretches out on the living room couch and raps on the window when he sees a masked Barry leaving a meal.

Barry starts and backs up. He stops and puts a hand over his heart.

Vihaan keeps his palm on the window even after Barry waves and leaves. After he retrieves the meal, he tries a little dancing, manages to sway back and forth, then waltzes across the room, three laps, before he sinks back onto the sofa. Maybe tomorrow he can do four laps.

Doris sends him a video of Italians sequestered but standing on their balconies, singing with their neighbors across the way. He watches it a dozen times, imagining and envying the comfort of not being alone.

He wonders how alone Rose felt as she faced her death. She'd been saddened by the people she knew who kept saying she was going to "beat it," by the people who refused to say goodbye. Before Vihaan was willing to admit the possibility of her death himself, he and Rose had an argument in which she'd said, "It's hard enough without you putting on blinders." She ran her hand over her bald head, soothing it, and then jumped to her feet. "My legs work, and I'm going on a walk." Vihaan had offered to go with her, but she'd said, "I can be alone. I am, and I will be." He'd tried to distract himself while she was gone, but as he paced from room to room, he had a vision of someone whizzing by in a car and shouting racial epithets at her. Only when he'd heard the front door open could he rest easy. He could not save her, save her from suffering. Surely, she, so forgiving, would have forgiven him.

His fever is down. He waltzes across the floor for five laps and bows to a nonexistent audience. A sudden thirst overwhelms him, and he gulps glass after glass of water. He has the hiccups for what seems like an hour, his diaphragm a skipping record, a tennis ball that keeps bouncing.

In the middle of the night, he opens the front door and allows himself to stand on the lawn. This is the first fresh air he's breathed in many days now. In moonlight glow, he sees flowers in Cliff's yard and misses the sturdy persistence of the backyard oak at West House. An ant crawls across his bare foot, the first living thing he's touched since he began quarantine. He holds out an arm as if reaching to grasp the hands of, to form a chain with, other afflicted people. They are part of a fellowship now, he and these strangers. It's surreal that mere weeks ago, everyone was walking around barefaced, ignorant. He lets his arm fall because it's too heavy, the same arm that has made countless serves. His bicep, which used to feel as hard as a deck of playing cards, seems to have melted and is sloshing around under his skin. He paces around the lawn, the grass plush beneath his feet.

The next day, his body quiets down, and he goes through long stretches without it claiming so much of his attention. He initiates a phone call to Will and is able to ask questions about how Will is, and the answers adhere to his memory. He feels less groggy.

He can tolerate the weight of artificial light again and stays up after sunset instead of just closing his eyes and drifting off. He reads the old *New Yorkers* that have been fanned across the coffee table, collecting dust. They are all pre-epidemic with no hint of what's to come.

A couple of more Blursdays, and he's fever free, can breathe more deeply. He shaves for the first time in however long, the newly exposed skin chilly, goose-bumped.

The doctor pronounces him ready to rejoin his people.

He dresses in his shorts and polo, happily crumpling into a ball the sweat-caked T-shirt and boxers he'd been wearing since he started in quarantine and zipping it into an outside pocket of his suitcase. Doris and Barry come to retrieve him. Vihaan and Doris fall into each other's arms, and he tries to breathe in her scent but still can't smell anything. Doris covers his heart with her palm as they huddle together in one of the Odyssey's back rows. They interweave their fingers.

At home, each roommate steps tentatively into Vihaan's personal space, either to hug him, squeeze his arm, or grasp his hand. He exhales.

While his smell and taste are on hiatus, he makes extra use of his other senses. He runs his hands over the furniture and counters. He sits in the backyard petting Ginger Rogers and listens to the birds singing. When he pays attention, he hears an almost constant soundtrack of birds communicating, a "ta-da, ta-da" of mourning doves. He notices the bright trim on the houses that he walks past on his way to the tennis court. With his rusty muscles and battered lungs, he can't walk all the way there yet, but he will.

Chapter 18: Surrender

JANE'S MAD AT herself that she hasn't adopted a dog. She'd had plenty of time to look before the pandemic, time also to convince the roommates of the benefits of canine company. Still, she's been afraid of the cost, and she's scared of the attachment. She distrusts her ability to choose a dog that will behave, that won't break her heart. What if her hands become shakier again, and she can't hold tight to a leash, and the dog dashes into the street and gets hit by a car?

She'd gritted her teeth for decades as a vet, willed the steeliness of mind to help the ailing animals as they flailed and moaned, and now she is both so hardened and so shredded that the prospect of adoption triggers an unpleasant tingle at the back of her throat and her shoulders creep toward her ears. As she reminds herself that she hasn't made a commitment, and that she won't make one, her shoulders float downward, her throat quiets.

She joins David at his house to watch a moody series about a boy's disappearance. The rest of the household has declared a moratorium on darkness in what they watch since there's enough of it in the news, in the air. David's house is refreshingly spare, most surfaces bare, with Tomás's Sagrada Familia a baroque exception. David has a tea caddy that he presents to Jane before each episode, and she's rotating through the herbals. She likes the effortless way he pours the tea water into the solid ceramic mugs, the rose pink of which has been designated as hers. She settles herself in one of the two comfy chairs with an ottoman, uses one of the two side tables. Occasionally, Jane drifts off during the show. When she wakes up and confesses, David rewinds.

After the show, they spend time sifting through the clues, issuing observations, guessing what will come next. One of the characters works in a daycare, and David mentions that he did so when he was in college. She can imagine David, with his long, gentle fingers, pushing a toddler in a swing.

Once, she awakens in his living room to find the room dark, the TV off. As she slept, David had spread a light blanket over her, and she has it bunched around her hands like cushy mittens. The chair creaks when she stands up somewhat unsteadily, and David emerges from his bedroom dressed in pajama bottoms, an oversized T-shirt, and flip-flops. He insists on walking her back to her house, and she threads her arm through his en route.

It doesn't hurt to look, Jane tells herself as she begins browsing dog adoption websites. Oh, Mr. Softee, with those soulful eyes. Agatha, her tail a plume, her ears cocked. Pierre (not a poodle) has a generous belly, primed for tickling. If any of these dogs appeared on her doorstep, she'd take it in.

She looks up from her laptop to the woefully empty street. Alas, no strays, and she wouldn't be surprised if a tumbleweed rolled down the street. Their cul-de-sac is quiet as a rule, but since the pandemic started, the waves of cars on nearby streets have thinned. At other times, the traffic slowdown would be welcome. Now each dwelling seems like a bunker. With everyone at home for more hours, Jane and her housemates bump into each other more. Someone is always in the living room with her, and she contemplates asking if each person could have some alone time there, but she doesn't want to come across as controlling.

After Amy died, she'd feared she'd rattle around by herself for the rest of her life. Back at her old house, when Barry and other friends had come over, she delayed their leaving by asking them one more question, by suggesting one more drink. "Tell me that story again," she'd say, "the one about …" Amy's addiction had made Amy never grow up, never really leave the nest, and Jane had felt a guilty comfort in not having to let go of her. She had more time with Amy than many parents end up having with their kids.

At this moment, however, she wants to be alone, far from Ellen clearing her throat in the kitchen, from the water pounding as someone takes a shower, from Barry humming tunelessly as he sits nearby, exuding heat. She closes her eyes, and she and Mr. Softee are entwined in a hammock on a third-story deck with views of boundless undulating hills and pointillist aspen, a place she's never been and will never go. In her daydream, she even has the abdominal strength necessary to get in and out of the hammock easily when she or Mr. Softee fancy a snack or a drink. His fur ruffles in the breeze.

She spills her tea on purpose to see how David reacts. She's chosen a climactic moment in the show. He pauses the episode, wipes up the fluid, and has a new cup brewing for her in no time.

She thinks of the care he takes of the semi-feral cat colony. She's seen him on bended knee near the cats, getting down to their height, respecting their space but rewarding their approaches with tender pets.

During a dog food commercial, he appears rapt. A dog and its human are playing Frisbee. "I need more exercise," he says.

"Missing playing tennis with Vihaan." He steeples his fingers. "So glad he's safe and sound. That was a scare."

"He's sound enough. Scared the shit out of me," Jane says.

David, never having heard her curse, lets out a whoop of laughter. "We're going to need a new show when this one ends," he says.

She realizes she'd been afraid of a time coming when she wouldn't have an excuse to escape to David's. She scooches down in the chair, settling in for the rest of the episode, and she feels a sensation as if a leash is slipping through her hand, but she lets it go because David is nearby. He's alert, his reflexes quick, and his hands steady. He'll pick up the slack.

Surely if David wanted a dog, he would have one. Still, she's gathered enough evidence to convince herself that he would make a great companion to a great companion. Now to persuade him.

The next night, after she and David make their predictions about what will happen on their show, she has an opportunity to broach the subject of adoption with him. Instead, she finds herself silent and dry mouthed, swept away by a memory of when she brought up the potential of having children with her then-girlfriend. The girlfriend, with a look of disgust, had said, "You want to be a breeder? Not me." It was as if Jane had been driving along merrily, imagining her girlfriend was content in the passenger seat, but it turned out the girlfriend had her own car and driver's seat and had just sideswiped her, spraying a confetti of glass. As Jane picked out the glass embedded in her skin, she'd proceeded on her own path as if she didn't owe the girlfriend a discussion, as if she could hide from her.

Over the years, it was a conscious chore for Jane to recognize that other people had their own agendas, their own dreams.

"What does this other person want?" became an item on her how-to-behave-like-a-better-person checklist. Still, she couldn't help but envision a dog's chin resting on David's knee, a little more warmth in this cold, cold time.

After the next episode of the show is over at David's, she asks, "What about a dog?"

"What about one?"

"For you. Good company, help you get more exercise."

David frowns, avoids her eye. "My ex called me 'selfish.'"

"Why's that?"

"I didn't want to spend the money on a pet. I've got a strict budget for retirement." He looks at his shoes as though ashamed of himself.

Jane sighs. "I certainly understand that."

"I also didn't want to attach myself to a creature bound to die before I do." He meets her eye for a moment, then starts to shred the paper napkin next to his tea mug.

"Understood." Maybe he could afford a dog if he didn't buy paper napkins and fancy teas, she thought. He doesn't need to subscribe to the special streaming service through which they've been watching their show. Her disappointment saps the strength she could use to lighten up the conversation, to forgive him for not wanting what she wants.

"I sometimes wish I were different," he says.

After she allows herself a silent "I wish you were too," she says, "I get a little tired of myself sometimes. I even started being a yenta, looking at dogs online, just in case you wanted some help."

David laughs with surprise, the way he did when he'd first heard her curse. "I can't remember anyone ever trying to fix me up. With a dog, no less." He rolls the napkin shreds into a ball.

As she says good night, she hugs him for the first time.

Tucked into bed, Jane has an idea. They can volunteer together, she and David. They could walk dogs, pet them, hug them. It won't cost them a cent. But they're in an epidemic, and who knows what kind of contact one would need to have when volunteering. Better play it safe. Soon she has the light on, and the image of Mr. Softee flickers on her computer. She magnifies the image, trying to make it more real, but it does hurt to look, to see what will never have a third dimension for her.

Amy's old therapist had been trying to help Amy develop healthier self-soothing techniques. Well, that was an abysmal failure, but it's not too late for Jane. She can use her imagination, so instead of gazing at Mr. Softee to take the edge off, she unclenches her jaw as she watches, behind her closed eyelids, a home movie in which David cartwheels, over and over, a continuous, comforting circle, a new friend for a bleak time. The soles of David's feet flashing through the air look like they're embedded with sparklers.

She fumbles but manages to switch off the bedside light while she still has her eyes closed, surrendering to the unknown.

Chapter 19: Old Reliable

It's not as though Barry was doing that much before COVID hit. Still. After the waves of death began, Barry's worrying about Vihaan and making meals for him had consumed him until Vihaan's state became less critical. Now, he has an hour-long debate with himself each morning about the need to get out of bed. He feels like an empty vending machine, and he pulls at his eyebrows as if they don't belong on his face.

The only thing he can make himself do each day, aside from his chores, is walk to the nearest moonlight tower, that metal behemoth of long-reaching streetlights. There he stretches his arms as far up as he can and grips the tower bars as if he were in a cage. He presses the metal until it makes grooves in his palms. A couple of pedestrians cross to the other side of the street, maybe just a COVID do-si-do, or maybe he looks unpredictable and they want to keep a safe distance for that reason. On the way back to the house, he wanders through the elementary school playground, which is empty and deflated. He attempts a pull-up on a bar, but he can barely hang on, let alone lift his ponderous weight.

He and Cliff are taking a break. Each of them had been single for so long that their togetherness had been turning from pleasantly surprising to somewhat stifling. At least that's what Cliff implied when he sat Barry down for a talk, and Barry found himself agreeing reluctantly.

He takes a slow jog, a slog, around the elementary school track and ends up with a stitch in his side. His running style provoked the other boys in elementary school to call him a "faggot," and at the time he'd had no idea what the word meant.

It's Barry's turn to make dinner. On a sheet pan, he fashions pork chops into a diamond shape, crisscrossed with a lower-case "t" of pearl onions. Ellen asks if the shape is the head of a kite. Doris declares it to be a crossroads. "It's a Rorschach meal," Barry says as he spears a ring of grilled pineapple. He fingers his cheek and is surprised by razor stubble. When had he last shaved or, for that matter, looked at himself in the mirror? Back in New York, he'd banished five-o'clock shadow by shaving twice a day, even on his days off.

The next day at the gloomy playground, he holds onto the bar and keeps his feet off the ground until it feels as if his underarms are ripping apart. Until this moment, he's never seen the appeal of masochism, but the bracing pain is so much more vibrant than the dazed and leaden fog in which he's been crouching.

At the moonlight tower, he lifts his knee and leans into the structure. If he were strong enough to use the metal crossbars to lift himself off the pavement, he could start climbing. He's not able to right now, but maybe he can work his way up to it.

Once when he was a boy, he and his older siblings had taken a hike. They'd scampered ahead of him on their long legs, and he lost sight of them. He'd had to run up the steep trail, not knowing which way to go at a fork, tripping and skinning his knees and hands. He'd allowed himself to cry, and the hot tears warmed him as the breeze grew bitter. Finally, he heard his sister calling his name, and he followed the sound of her voice until he caught up. He promised not to tell their parents that the siblings had left him behind, and his sister rewarded his discretion with a cookie.

Now he can't rely on hearing a voice calling him from the right direction, guiding him, though he wishes for one.

***

As Barry goes through his morning getting-out-of-bed debate, he hears a tap on his door. He almost says, "Go away" but forces a "Give me a minute," in which he dons some shorts and rubs sleep from his eyes.

It's Tomás, and he says, "Confession," as he takes a seat at the edge of Barry's bed.

Barry nods.

"You know how the world might end, and it might not matter what we do right now?" Tomás asks.

"That's one way to look at it." A way that sounds familiar now that Tomás is putting it into words. "What's the problem?"

"I've been getting reacquainted with the spirits." The skin under Tomás's bleary eyes is elephant gray.

"You're getting religion?" Barry is surprised, almost jealous.

Tomás sighs a gust of sour air. "No, of course not. I've been having a nip here and there."

"Ahhh." Barry flashes on an image of Tomás choosing to jump from the tower on 9/11 rather than be devoured by the flames. He feels impatient with Tomás's self-destructiveness but checks his own conscience for spots of mold, for self-pity.

He'd been hoping to hide his distress from his housemates, to uphold his reputation of being the cheerful one, the old, reliable one. Maybe if he tells Tomás about his own battles, they can both have someone else's problems to focus on.

First step, Barry orders, is for Tomás to pour his secret stash down the toilet.

Second step, they agree, is for Barry to take Tomás to the playground, where they both struggle on the bars. The ripping feeling as Barry forces himself to dangle in the air seems a degree less intense than it had been. When he lets go, his shoulders are slick with sweat from the effort.

They amble over to the moonlight tower. Barry throws an arm around it and introduces it to Tomás as if it's a friend they're meeting for lunch.

"You're more screwed up than I am," Tomás says. He tilts back his head.

"Beg to differ."

"I can see the charm," Tomás says, patting the intricate structure.

Tomás comes to Barry's room again the following morning. He digs into his shorts and reveals a fifth, and Barry ushers Tomás out the door to the bathroom. Barry stands outside the closed door, and a few moments later, he hears a flush. He taps on the door and asks, "Done in there?"

"All right. All right." There's another flush.

Tomás emerges and goes out to hide the bottle in the recycling. He returns to the kitchen, wiping his hands on his shorts. "Excursion after breakfast?" he offers.

On the way to the playground, Barry asks, "So, I'm keeping your secret?"

Tomás nods. "Ellen knew about my first drink but hasn't asked about it since." He kicks a stone down the sidewalk.

"That's a lousy excuse, you know."

"Doesn't she have enough to worry about?" Tomás asks.

Barry nods. Down the block, in the middle of the road, three enormous buzzards hunch over roadkill. Barry thinks about how in New York, they've been fashioning temporary graves and mass burial sites in the scramble for how to deal with the COVID dead. Barry closes his eyes, feels woozy, then snaps open his eyes. He reminds himself that his job is just to make it through the day, not to figure out what to do with corpses.

At the playground, kids gallop around, using the play structures as an obstacle course, zigging and zagging. A youngster easily polishes off chin-ups as another kid keeps count, "Twenty-nine, thirty …"

At the moonlight tower, Barry hugs the metal, though he'd really like to hug Tomás. No, the person he'd most like to hug is Cliff. He wants to feel Cliff's chest solid against his, to feel Cliff's chin resting on his shoulder, the brick of heat they create together.

"Cliff and I are taking a break."

Tomás pats his shoulder. "You've been looking a bit sad."

Barry grips the tower's metal and strains as hard as he can to lift himself, to get a foothold on the structure. In Barry's daydream, Tomás plants his feet and aids in pushing Barry up from behind. Barry's up off the ground, on the first rung of a giant's baroque ladder. He hauls himself up to the next level, every muscle straining but obeying as if life depends on it. Tomás cheers, "We can do it!" and the "we" seems right. Though Barry can't climb the moonlight tower any farther, in his mind, he's climbing a pyramid, the Empire State Building, the Eiffel Tower, with no ropes or special equipment except many decades of living and listening. If he were at the top of the moonlight tower, he could look down at the sidewalk, the squares of it as small as dominos, Tomás's upturned beaming face the size of a thumbnail. Up top, he could run his hands over the smooth glass of the enormous light bulbs. It would be lonely and soothing to have escaped gravity to that extent.

Time is standing still, and Tomás seems to be waiting for a response from Barry. "I'm sad, yes," Barry says, but he's smiling. The playground is still there for his clumsy attempts at pull-ups, for glimpses of just how stubborn he can be.

All that's left of the vultures' meal of roadkill is a blood stain on the dirty tablecloth of asphalt. In time, it will rain, and even the stain will vanish for those who didn't see the carnage.

Chapter 20: Untold

EVERY TIME THE doorbell rings, Pearl's afraid that it might be Ruby. Not that they're answering the doorbell right now, anyway. The bell is invariably for grocery delivery, and they wave to the delivery person, with the window serving as a barrier, so their exhalations don't mingle. Before opening the front door, they wait a few minutes, what seems a sufficient amount of time for germs to dissipate. If Pearl is lugging in grocery sacks, she holds her breath when she's on the doorstep.

Pearl has rehearsed what she would say if Ruby came by. "Ruby, I'm so sorry, but we've made a household decision not to have anyone come inside." Pearl has no obligation to tell Ruby about Cliff and David having golden tickets. Ruby's responses vary in Pearl's imagination. In one scenario, Ruby says, "Wow. Should have figured …" and flips Pearl the bird before turning on her heel and stomping away. In another version, Ruby says, "I understand completely. I just wanted to wave from a distance and thank you for all you've already done for me." In a third possibility, Ruby doesn't say a thing and waits for Pearl to explain herself further, but Pearl has no words, only a coughing fit that sends Ruby on her way as if Pearl had just reached out and slapped her with her hacking noises.

She'd thought she'd welcome a break from work, but this pandemic vacation has become the longest time off from a job she's had since she was in her teens. Retirement is for other people. Who is she if she isn't helping someone?

Pearl's doctor won't refill her blood pressure and cholesterol meds unless she goes in for a lab visit. She complains about the risk of being in a medical setting, but Doris bullies her into going, citing the risk of Pearl not having the medicine. Doris and Vihaan volunteer to take her, and as they enter the parking lot, rain is pouring down, and a woman wearing a garbage bag as a raincoat is huddling under the awning of a shuttered restaurant. Pearl squints as if greater focus will help her read the woman's facial features that are still exposed to the air: a blurry nose, wet furrowed forehead. Maybe the swollen ankles and duct-taped sneakers are Ruby's.

When they park for the lab, a few hundred feet from the huddled woman, Pearl hopes that Maybe-Ruby hasn't spotted them. She double-masks and keeps her chin down, an umbrella obscuring her further.

As the phlebotomist is drawing her blood, Pearl feels surprised that the blood in the tube belongs to her, that it flows out of sight, just doing its unsung job. "Are you all right, ma'am?" asks the phlebotomist. "You're awfully white."

This strikes Pearl as funny, and her laugh comes out as a gurgle, as if she were underwater.

When Pearl returns to the car, Maybe-Ruby is nowhere to be seen, though a few shopping bags remain where she'd been. Pearl digs in the glove compartment for a few of the baggies of loose change they keep there to give to street people. She asks Vihaan to stop by the cluster of shopping bags. When she gets out of the car, she smells a familiar smell, though maybe that's just the smell that lingers from anyone who hasn't bathed in a while. She drops the baggies of change, which land with a satisfying thud, as if they are imbued with more value than they actually have. She hastens back into the getaway car, and Vihaan steps on the gas.

"What was that about?" Doris asks.

"Earlier there was a person there. She looked kind of like Ruby, but I couldn't tell for sure."

"I wonder how she is," Vihaan says. "Her life seemed hard enough before all of this …"

Pearl sees her reflection in the car window and realizes she's still masked. Her eyes look hollow, and the rivulets of rain dripping down the window might be tears.

Two weeks earlier, Ruby's friend from their latest campsite persuaded a passerby to call 911. Ruby was radiating heat, and her skin had a bluish tint. No one wanted to get too close to her in case she had what Ruby's friends are calling the "plague." None of them visited the hospital after she was admitted, both because they weren't allowed to and they were afraid.

Here's what an obituary might have said had it been written by those who cared for her, had those who cared for her known more of her history:

> Ruby Garces, age 75, died of COVID. She did not go peacefully.
>
> As a young child growing up in Brownsville, she amused herself by spinning in circles until she fell down. She trained herself to run backwards and was faster at it than anyone she knew. Her mother called her "Squirt." At the age of 7, Ruby saw *The Wizard of Oz* for the first time; later, when she had a VCR, she watched *The Wizard* every Friday night for years. Each

viewing included the downing of a bag of microwaved popcorn.

When Ruby was a high school freshman, she lost her parents and a sister to a drunk driver. Her two older brothers raised her by holding down construction jobs that exhausted them but paid the bills. After losing more than half her family, the only thing that made sense to Ruby was to buckle down at school, where effort seemed to equal outcome. She would be the first family member to go to college. At UT in Austin, she felt self-conscious and would rarely speak up in classes. In Brownsville, she hadn't had to work to make friends because she'd known her classmates her whole life. In Austin, she grew apart from her one hometown friend when the friend found a boyfriend. When Ruby was growing up, she didn't know the term "asexual," but it was comforting to her to learn, much later, that she wasn't the only one. At UT, Ruby majored in philosophy, wanting to know what the great thinkers thought, what reality is, why we're here, how to think about thinking. Her studies raised more questions and, thus, served their purpose.

After college, Ruby found a job proofreading state legislation. She worked in the basement of the Capitol in an office with a seasonal cricket infestation and no windows. Over the years she had a number of jobs. At each, she would stay until she felt suicidal and decided that the job was not worth her life. In a mad scramble, she'd find another job that was just intended as a bridge to something better, a stopgap because she never had enough savings to coast without another job already lined up. Her rent rose more quickly than her wages.

She didn't drive because, though her brothers had tried to persuade her to learn, she was too afraid. The prospect of injuring another person with a car was unbearable.

When she worked as a cook at the coffee shop, she left the house before dawn. The restaurant was a little more than a twenty-minute walk. Sometimes she'd skip a few blocks, gasping for breath in a pleasant way. Once a man darted toward her from behind a building, and she ran as fast as she could, sobbing, until she arrived at work, safe enough. Her boss bought her pepper spray and a self-defense class.

In her prime, she lent money to her brothers and friends without the expectation of getting it back. She checked in with elderly neighbors. On her coworkers' half-birthdays, she gave them homemade cupcakes with cream-cheese frosting.

Underinsured, she racked up medical bills for migraines and gum disease. She stopped giving away money and baking cupcakes. She no longer made medical appointments. Her VCR broke.

If she had a day off and the season was right, she walked down to the Capitol Avenue Bridge at twilight to see the colony of bats fly out from under the bridge, swaths of them, unfurling across the sky, a speckled carpet. In other seasons, she waited until evening, donned her fluorescent green runner's vest, and strolled past the orange and yellow lights glowing in other people's windows. She patted the pepper spray in her front pocket. Sometimes she thought it would be okay if someone took her and just disappeared her, a vague, bloodless death—not because she wanted to die, but because she was content with the life she'd had.

Homelessness came after missed buses, missed work, missed bills, missed rental payments. Her brothers both said she could live with them, but she politely declined. The money she made selling her furniture on Craigslist—"Everything Must Go!"—bought her a sleeping bag, a tent, a sturdy backpack for her changes of clothes, and a couple more months of having plenty to eat before she started asking for money, food, and occasional shelter on the coldest nights of the year.

Shout-outs to those friends who kept her company on walks, who sung "Over the Rainbow" with her, who shared a meal, shared a thought, shared a feeling, shared a laugh. One friend would walk backwards with her, keeping a few feet ahead of Ruby to catch her if she fell.

Thank you to the public library, to public restrooms, and to drinking fountains.

Several weeks before Ruby contracted COVID, Ginger the Cat was sitting on the front porch. A woman who'd come to the house before on a dozen or so occasions approached. She made a clicking noise and held her hand out to Ginger, who came forward for a pet. After a bit, the woman turned around and walked away, and she became a dappled shadow behind Ginger's closed eyes. None of the humans were aware of Ruby's visit.

Chapter 21: Smudges

Ellen knows Tomás has been up to something. The cash they keep in a desk drawer has been disappearing, with no explanation for where the money is going. Plus, Tomás has been sounding more thick-tongued, slower. Waves of vacancy pass over his face. She wants to shake him. Sometimes she feels their marriage is a series of hurdles over which they've stumbled, continuing the obstacle course without learning how to jump.

Tomás's relationship to alcohol had seemed resolved decades ago. She knew that alcoholics who stopped drinking sometimes still called themselves alcoholics, and this must be why. At any moment, Tomás could pass through the rotting doorway to that dusty room that has always been there, waiting for him, a room with withered arms beckoning.

She picks up the phone. It's been at least a few years since they've spoken. She'd thought about calling Geoff when she was diagnosed with cancer. Way back when, he'd been the first man to ever see her breasts, his touch so light, as if they were breakable. He too is a place that has always been there for her to reenter—but not a sordid, spooky room, as Ellen imagines the room full of alcohol that awaited Tomás's misstep. Talking to Geoff used to always bring her back to the room in which she'd first known him. He had a plaid cotton blanket on the simple pine twin bed in which they'd lay braided together, she inhaling the whisper of lemony aftershave on his cheek. From the bed, she could see the rest of the furniture: a plain desk with a drawer full of fresh sharpened pencils, a squat dresser polished with Pledge, a floor lamp with an ivory shade the same color as his sheets. He was the only student she'd known who had matching furniture. She'd broken up with Geoff when Tomás came along.

She puts down the phone. If she still feels like talking with Geoff tomorrow, she'll call. Of course, it's possible he's no longer alive. Or what if he's going to die tomorrow and this is her chance to say goodbye? On the other hand, is it presumptuous to think she'd be on the list of people he'd want to spend time with on the day before he died? Certainly, his wife (if she's still around), his kids, his grandkids, his beloved golden retriever (was the current one named Ollie?) would be higher up on the list, and she'd only be imposing. Still, Geoff must have caller ID and could screen his calls.

She distracts herself by refreshing her email. One email is from a widower to whom she's sent a drawing of his wife, based on her obituary picture in the local newspaper. He thanks her profusely and has attached a few more images. "Today is her birthday," writes the widower. Ellen sharpens her colored pencils and spends the afternoon trying to capture the woman's playful demeanor. She ends up crumpling numerous sheets of paper. It's so hard to portray someone's light. At last, she's satisfied with one of the drawings and sends it with a simple, "You must miss her spark."

Ellen's chore today is vacuuming. As she moves around the house, sucking up a cobweb here, a crumpled leaf there, she wishes for a way to vacuum her mind of ruminations, or maybe the ruminations move too fast to be swept up in a vacuum. She needs instead a flyswatter and a swift hand.

"You keep going over that same spot," says Doris, who's sitting on the sofa observing. "Are you okay?"

Ellen realizes that searching Tomás's face for signs of drunkenness had so preoccupied her at breakfast and lunch that she'd only eaten a few bites. Her body is no longer used to restricting food intake, and her blood sugar is so low that she barely makes it to the couch in time to slump onto it. Doris hustles to the kitchen and returns to the sofa with a glass of apple juice. She watches until Ellen, her hands shaking, finishes it.

The next day Ellen picks up the phone. She remembers early in her marriage when she used to call Geoff and complain about Tomás, about his drinking, about how he left the household chores to her.

"Ah, you could have stayed with me. I'm still free," Geoff said more than once, to which she'd had no reply. They'd had phone sex back before they'd ever heard a term for it. He said he'd wait for her, but he did get married and didn't want to talk with her at first. After that, her kids were young, and she didn't return his phone calls, afraid that talking to him might make her want to run away. Before becoming a parent, she'd seen her relationship with Geoff as a relief valve, making it possible to stay with Tomás. Those first few years of parenting while trying to keep her real estate practice thriving had worn her out so much that she imagined her conversations with Geoff would push her to abandon the family for whatever dregs married Geoff might offer or, in another fantasy, she'd create her own witness protection program in which she'd resettle under a different name in a studio apartment within walking distance of an ocean or Great Lake. Tomás was such a wonderful father that she both trusted that he'd do fine without her and wanted to stick it out with him and the kids because he provided the marvelous glue that she felt should inspire her.

The closest she'd come to running away had been when she was in her thirties. She told Tomás she was attending a conference, and she flew to Nashville, where Geoff lived. He was still married to his first wife at the time, but he spent all day in Ellen's hotel room with her. They turned up the air conditioning to wick off the sweat they created, and they ordered Bloody Marys and grilled cheese through room service. Around six each evening, Geoff left, and she was happy to see him go, both because of her too-full belly, which she associated with his presence, and because of the wave of guilt that caught up with her by the end of the day.

Abruptly aware of the smudges on her phone, Ellen goes to the bathroom, finds an alcohol wipe, and dabs at the phone. She thinks of the trysts that she had after Geoff as smudges on her character that she managed to wipe clean by rationalizing that they were meaningless distractions, like impulse buys that get shoved to the back of a closet, later to be donated, unused, to Goodwill.

Now that the phone is clean, she is ready to use it. When he picks up, she announces herself, her voice a bit shaky.

"Ellen who?" He sounds genuinely puzzled.

"Ellen Ellen." She almost says, "Your Ellen," but instead says, "It's me, Geoff."

"Oh, yes," he says, still sounding unsure.

"I wanted to see how you are. What with COVID and everything …"

"I have a daughter. Her name is Deidre, and she's a doctor. She got sick, and now she can barely climb a set of stars. I mean, a set of stairs."

"I remember you having a daughter." Ellen's eyes are burning. Deirdre was Geoff's first wife's name; his daughter's name is Elena.

"You do?"

"She went to medical school in Galveston."

"Ah, yes. You do know us. You might have to remind me who you are. Are you Deirdre's friend? I'm forgetting things these days."

"I'm your old friend Ellen." She will not be telling him all she wants to tell him. He would have said about her cancer, "You poor, sweet thing. You must be so worried." He would have been pleased that she was eating normally. He would have asked her all about her new living situation in the co-op. He would have inquired with caution about Tomás. When he heard that she was worried Tomás was drinking again, he would have sighed and suggested that she just talk to him. That was always his suggestion, just talk to Tomás. He couldn't see how hard it was for her.

"You and I went to college together," Ellen says. She imagines her words as a dart, sticking for a moment to the dartboard, then sliding to the floor.

"Oh, yes. Tell me your name again."

"Ellen."

She hears a snuffling sound from his end and a dog yipping in the background. "Are you the one who broke my heart?" he asks. "More than once?"

Her first impulse is to disconnect the phone, and her hand starts to shake. "That would be me," she says. "I'm so, so sorry. You wouldn't believe how sorry I am."

She hears him mutter, "Good girl." The golden retriever might have been Molly, not Ollie, or maybe this is a new one. "Can you say it again?" he asks. "Tell me again, please, what you just told me."

"I'm that Ellen. Please forgive me."

That room that she's been thinking is hers for the entering is now roped off, like a room in a museum that is undergoing preparation for a new exhibit. She's sneaked under the rope, lain down on Geoff's college bed a last time, this time alone, before it's put in storage.

***

She talks to Tomás about his drinking that evening, and he admits it.

"What are you going to do about it?" she asks.

He sits speechless.

"I don't want to be a cop." She's exhausted, and she's got another scan coming up that's worrying her. Maybe the cancer has been thrumming in the background all along, and maybe if Geoff had been all right, he would have guessed whether or not she still had cancer over the phone.

"I kicked it before," Tomás says. "I'll see if I can enlist Barry. He likes playing cop, and I think he needs a project."

She shakes his hand, then clasps it between hers. It's enough for now. She adjourns to the living room, where she finds the day's newspaper and reads the obituaries, making new acquaintances.

Chapter 22: Melting

When Doris was in the high school classroom during the lockdown, she'd promised herself that if she got out alive, she'd be more appreciative of all she'd taken for granted. Each day, she's been taking a minute to savor a single raisin, a practice in which Vihaan joined when he recovered from COVID. They sit with the raisins on top of their tongues, squirreled in their cheeks, rolling around their mouths. The raisins' skins melt, and they are left with the slick innards. They sit facing each other, one of them occasionally sticking out their tongue to show off their prize.

When raisin time is over this morning, she has a message from the counselor at the school where she'd subbed on that awful day. A dozen of the students from that class have been meeting online as a group under the counselor's supervision, and they've expressed concern about how she's faring. Would she like to join for one of their Zoom sessions? Yes, she would. As she's emailing the necessary confidentiality documents to the counselor, she makes a request of the students, which the counselor agrees to pass on.

For the first time since the pandemic flared—that wildfire that is nowhere near under control—Doris dresses up. She wears lipstick, a blouse instead of a T-shirt, and pants with a zipper instead of pull-ons. It feels odd to be doing this Zoom meeting from her bedroom, but it's the only place in the house where she can have a confidential conversation. She has trouble finding a spot to talk that won't reveal her bed in the background, but she unlocks her desk's casters, wheels it to the center of the room, then sits in the desk's usual place with the shaded window behind her.

She has signed into the meeting as "Doris, She/Her" though the students had known her as Ms. Bennett. The experience they shared broke the shell of formality between she and them, as far as she's concerned. Still, one of them greets her, "Hey, miss," and another "It's good to see you, ma'am."

"Call me Doris, please," she says.

They don't all have their audio on, but she reads a few of the students' lips as they try her name out. She may be the first Doris they've ever known; it's a name that has gone the way of Lois and Phyllis.

"We were wondering how you're doing," says the student with whom she'd mimed exchanging glasses of water.

"Well, I've had some nightmares since that day," she says.

"Me, too," a few of them chime in.

"I'm glad we're doing school all online," says one of the students, her hair obscuring her eyes. "It's safer this way. I never have to go out."

The counselor says to the student, "You had made going for a walk a goal of yours this week."

"Couldn't do it," the student says. "Got outside. There was nowhere to hide, and I thought my heart was going to burst until I went back inside."

"Ah, that makes me sad," says Doris. "But it's good you tried."

Another student, broad shouldered, says, "To me, I can breathe better outside. There's somewhere to run away. Space. I'm not trapped."

"Doris, how are you spending your free time?" asks one of the students.

She hadn't expected the question. "Well, I miss my weekly folk dancing, and I used to like to go to the bakery and make a cinnamon roll last an hour. Still, I share a house with six other people, and we hang out, make meals, go for walks."

"Your kids and grandkids?" asks the interviewing student.

"Just old friends."

"My parents are polyamorous," announces the young woman who doesn't want to go outside. "I have two dads and a mom."

"I could use a spare dad," says the interviewing student.

Ms. Villareal, the counselor, says, "Do you remember what Ms. Bennett was hoping to hear today?"

A student who's been quiet until this point says, "I'll go first." A cappella, she belts out a song about dying birds. Her voice is so piercing, in a good way, that Doris recalls the TV commercials in which Ella Fitzgerald holds a note that breaks glass.

At the end of the song, everyone puts on their mics and applauds. Doris leads the standing ovation. When a couple of the students stand, it turns out they're only wearing underwear from the waist down.

"What the hell, Jasmine?" asks one of the students. "I didn't know you could sing. I mean, really sing."

Jasmine's face is suffused with pink, and her eyes are brimming.

"Jasmine, you should enter a contest," another student says. "Miss—I mean, Doris—did you want us to sing our favorite song or just play it? I'm not prepared to sing. I might be prepared on, say, the first day of never."

"Oh, I just thought you could play a recording," Doris says. "That was such a special treat, Jasmine."

Doris doesn't recognize any of the songs the students play but finds some of them catchy and sways back and forth to the beat, as do a few students.

"I don't have anything," says Mario, the only student who hasn't said a peep so far. He hangs his head and rubs his eye with his fist, whispering something.

"I'm sorry, Mario, but could you speak up a little?" asks Ms. Villareal.

"*Mi abuelo* died this week. He had the disease."

The counselor and Doris jump in with their condolences, and the students follow.

Mario says, "There was a funeral gathering online, and they played a song he liked. Something about an unbroken circle and a better home waiting for the dead. I liked the circle image, but I think my *abuelo* was just fine with his home here. My sister was crying and rubbed her snotty nose on my shirt."

Doris doesn't believe in the better home awaiting either, but the song starts to play in her head. She wonders if she could sing it, though she decides against it, wanting instead to leave the space and time for the students. This is their therapy group, not hers. Also, she doesn't trust her singing to be in tune or thicker than a wisp. What's more, "Will the Circle Be Unbroken" is a religious song, and the students don't need that in school.

What had she most feared at their age? Nuclear war and getting pregnant. What would she have liked from a kind older person? For her passions and sorrows to be respected, and for that person to offer a simple way for her to break the rumination that had prevented her from getting enough sleep or from venturing out of her comfort zones. She'd been far from a carefree youth; she'd started every morning with her concealer stick, trying to hide the dark circles under her eyes and the stress zits on her chin. She'd picked her cuticles until they bled.

Doris asks, "Ms. Villareal, do we have a few minutes for an exercise?"

Ms. Villareal side-eyes her but gives her the go-ahead.

"Why don't y'all go to your kitchen and find something small, like a raisin, that you can try to dissolve in your mouth as slowly as possible?"

"Snack time!" says Jasmine.

Among the students' kitchen finds are a cheese cube, a small square of bread, a chocolate kiss, an ice cube, a Cheerio, a tortilla chip, and a spoonful of peanut butter. Doris has a trusty raisin.

"I'd like you to just let it float in your mouth. You might think about where it came from, what was involved in growing it or getting it to your kitchen. A team of people worked on conveying it to you. There was a natural occurrence in harmony with the people acting with intention." She feels a little woo-woo, unmasked, and it's liberating. "Something transformed. Like water into ice, corn into a chip. Let's be quiet while we let this piece of refreshment sit with us."

In Doris's room, light is creeping under the bottom of the window shade she's drawn. Light fell on the grape from which her raisin was born. Water sprinkled it. Then, under her closed eyelids, she sees the faces of the students as the humans who ushered this raisin to its final home, in this house. A human, maybe Jasmine, picked it. Another human drove it to a way station for processing. A human, or maybe a robotic arm, swept it into its canister, sealed it to preserve it. Another human put it on the shelf in the grocery store. Another human, maybe Mario, placed the canister in a grocery bag.

Doris's one-minute timer rings.

"My Cheerio, it just melted right away, but I could still taste it. Like it left some tasty dust."

A student plucks the cheese cube from his mouth and holds it up. "Still going strong. What was this for?"

"Just a pause," Doris says.

The student who said he likes to be outside, to get space, says, "My mom says I can't sit still these days. Always got a part of me tapping or jiggling. I don't want to slow down."

Ms. Villareal says, "Maybe that's your homework. See if anything bad happens if you quiet your body. Just for a minute."

Each student makes a modest goal for the week, and it's time for goodbyes. Doris exchanges thank yous with the group. One student is waving as the images melt from her computer screen.

She has a feeling of fullness, as if the raisin she's just savored contained the bulk and energy of a handful, so sweet, so deep.

Chapter 23: Downsizing

Tomás tilts his head back to see the top of the moonlight tower. His shoulder lightly touches Barry's, while Barry is in his own reverie, eyes shut, breathing labored. Sometimes Tomás wishes that affection between male friends was a custom in this country, that he could walk the streets holding Barry's hand, platonically, and no one would interpret this gesture as signifying something romantic or sexual. In this alternate world, he would now pick up Barry's hand and interlace fingers with him.

Tomás asks, "Are you going to reach out to Cliff? We could pop by his place."

"Too stalkerish."

"'We're just out for a walk, thought we'd say hello.'"

Barry holds up a hand as a stop sign. "Absolutely not."

Tomás wants to gift Barry something, and he recognizes the feeling as one from their past. Back when he, Barry, and Ellen had been a threesome, he'd felt the weight of being both Barry's and Ellen's favorite. He'd bestowed sexual attention on Barry as dutifully and mindlessly as he'd have fed a hungry pet. If he focused on Barry, Barry could feel loved, not left out. Then he wanted Barry to fade into the background because, indeed, Tomás had cared more to connect with Ellen.

Today Tomás doesn't want Barry to fade into the background. He wants to give Barry a gift that will bring back the

Barry sparkle, make him more present, lighten whatever load is dulling Barry's eyes and skin. Also, Tomás wants to think about something more constructive than how good cranberry juice would taste with a splash of vodka. It's been a few months since he stopped drinking, but he still has aftershocks. He has a vision of himself twenty years in the future. Ellen and all his friends have died, and he has rare visits from his kids and grandkids. The grandkids might have kids of their own. In his tiny apartment, he listens to Audible, or whatever the newer-fangled version of that will be, because his eyesight will be blurry. He will take up drinking again. The liquor store employees will know his name and deliver to his door; they will show, through their smiles and pats on his arm, that he deserves this alcoholic compensation for his long years of abstinence, for his losses. He will keep up his hand strength by opening the liquor bottles. This is a comforting vision.

But right now, his fabulous friend Barry is still alive, and Tomás wants to drink that in. He says the first thing that pops into his head.

"Barry, if you could open an envelope that told you the date you're going to die, would you?"

"That's kind of morbid."

Tomás feels a band of tension clamp his forehead, like a too tight hat. "We don't talk enough about dying, or getting older, for that matter. We're in the middle of a pandemic, and we're old."

"I'm not old. Old is later." Barry pushes off from the moonlight tower and beckons Tomás to follow.

"'Old' isn't an insult, a slippage. It's something we've achieved."

"Bah. Slow lap around the track?"

Tomás nods. "Like, say, you're going to die a year from now. Wouldn't it be good to get in touch with Cliff? He was kind of the icing on your cake."

A discarded dirtied mask is center sidewalk, and Barry kicks it into the grass. "Good cake doesn't need icing. Don't you remember when we did that weird ritual, putting something into the sinkhole? I said I wasn't going to settle for crumbs. He hasn't reached out, and that speaks volumes."

"Have you checked in with him? Maybe he's reading you the same way. A pity that would be, two stubborn old men."

They slog around the school track. Tomás experiments with raising his knees as high as possible, as if he were in a marching band. Barry trudges, barely lifting his feet from the ponderous ground. Tomás marches around Barry, encircling him. "Personal space," Barry says, at which point, Tomás trips over his own feet and knocks into Barry, who falls surprisingly easily to the ground, as if he were just waiting for a nudge. He lies face down on the track, not moving.

"Oh, crap, are you okay?"

Barry scrambles onto his elbows, his face red from exertion and road rash. "Sometimes you're a pain in the ass."

"I know. I annoy myself a lot of the time." It's a relief to admit this. Tomás hauls Barry up and gives him a clumsy hug, which Barry allows. "Are you hurt?"

"My face feels tender, but nothing else yet."

The hug with Barry gives Tomás a buzz, making him feel unexpectedly warm and snazzy. What has flickered across his daydreams and night dreams now and then these last fifty years—he, Ellen, and Barry together again—seems today like a solution. More love, less loss. He and Ellen could reunite with Barry.

"Maybe you're right," Barry says, and Tomás wonders if Barry has read his mind about how they could be closer again. "Maybe I ought to get in touch with Cliff. What have I got to lose?"

"Right." Tomás is disappointed. He tries to make his expression bright, enthusiastic.

He thinks of the miniatures he's continued to make and how much he's had to downsize his life with age, with the tight budget, with the pandemic. Now the miniatures are starting to take up too much space, encroaching on the area he needs to keep clear for creation.

The next day, he offers the roommates their choice of the miniatures. He gathers the rest, a few dozen, in a pillowcase and takes off on his mission. He wants to be the opposite of a porch pirate, a porch fairy. A dog barks at him from a living room window. He watches from across the street as a lithe young woman gets out of her car in the driveway and finds on her welcome mat the three-inch picnic table with its tiny benches and flowered tablecloth. He saves a few of the miniatures for the playground. He places one on a swing, one on top of the slide, one on the track. When the pillowcase is empty, he tucks it into his shirt collar, as if it were an enormous napkin, and does a few jumping jacks before he makes his way around the track until his legs feel weak, and he allows himself a rest, wiping his sweaty forehead with the pillowcase. A mourning dove cries nearby.

He will never have a piece of art in a world-class museum. He will never be pregnant or give birth. He will never know the date of his death sealed in that theoretical envelope unless he plans his death himself, which he has no intention of doing. He will never know what happened to the tissue that was scooped out of Ellen's breast. He will never know what Barry felt when they had that hug yesterday, nor will he know what Ellen feels when he gets home today and calls out, "Where's my Elly?"

Still, she'll appear from their bedroom, her hair damp and her red velvet robe on, and say, "I'm right here. Not going very far these days." Her hair will smell like coconut, he will find, as he buries his face in it.

She'll tug at the pillowcase now tucked into his waistband. "How did it feel to give it all away?"

"It felt right," he'll say. "Now I have some space."

Barry will be at the end of the hallway, looking brighter since he hung out with Cliff the night before. Tomás will consider throwing an arm around Barry, pulling him into the embrace he has with Ellen, but then he remembers that Barry wants personal space. Tomás can allow space to be empty without grasping to fill it up. He has gone another day without alcohol, and when he pictures his thirst, he sees the ripped blue discarded mask that he and Barry passed the other day. A good wind could pick it up, and he would not run after it. He would let it go.

Chapter 24: Antacids

Vihaan thought he would be better by now. The doctor says his lungs haven't healed. He's underweight because he still can't taste or smell much, he has intermittent waves of nausea, and food has become utilitarian. He can't play tennis with his students, so he teaches from the sidelines when he can find two students to play each other. He talks to Barry about his diminished income, and Barry lowers his rent. Doris has been filling in for him on his household chores when he's too exhausted. He has nightmares about having to live without some of his body parts—his eye, his leg, his dominant forearm. Part of the anguish of the nightmares is dealing with the pity and averted eyes of others.

He does have a new saving grace. He, Doris, his son, Will, and Will's boyfriend, Darrell, have been having biweekly Zoom dinners. The others are the chattiest, and he plays his part by nodding and interjecting questions if there's a lull. Will occasionally turns the computer camera to his ancient, ragged brown mutt who's looking frail on the couch, and Vihaan identifies with the dog. He never thought he'd go this long without seeing Will in person, but teleconferencing is a miracle, a salve. He wants to tell Rose that Will has found someone who loves and appreciates him. That hadn't happened yet when she died, and she'd worried. Doris notices after one of the calls that Will isn't drinking, though his boyfriend usually has a glass of red that he sips during the meals. During the Zoom dinners, Vihaan's symptoms fade into the background.

"I've got something to tell you," Will says one evening.

Vihaan's mind races to think what it might be. Will's getting married. They're having children. Vihaan grins at the prospects.

Darrell takes Will's hand. Will says, "It's about Uncle Sanjay," and a tear rolls from his eye.

Vihaan squints to make sure he's not mistaken. He tenses. "Tell me," he says almost reluctantly.

It takes Will a long time to speak. "He used to say I couldn't be your kid because I was too black. He said I didn't look like any of the family on your side. Wasn't as smart as any of you. Wasn't athletic like you. He'd wait until you and Mom were out of the room, and he'd hiss these things at me."

"That piece of shit!" Vihaan spits out with all the lung strength he can muster. He has a coughing fit.

"Is there something I should know?" asks Will. "I thought about taking one of those ancestry tests, but I was too scared."

"Of course, you're mine. Once your voice deepened, people used to mistake us on the phone for each other. Remember?"

"I guess that's true."

"And we both have these noses that look like they're broken."

Will is smiling now, and Darrell has an arm looped around his shoulder.

"Why didn't you bring this up before?" Vihaan asks.

"You and Mom always told me to ignore bullies. I thought I could. And I didn't want to be a snitch."

Vihaan pictures Will toughing it out with a pebble in his shoe all these years, telling himself to pay it no attention. "I'm so sorry," he says.

After they say goodnight, Vihaan has to lie down. What can he do with his anger at his brother now that Sanjay's dead? The same thing he did when he was alive. Swallow it. He remembers buying Sanjay a ticket to visit them in Tucson when Will was little. Sanjay behaved as if Rose and Will were invisible. He didn't lift a finger to help with the meals, didn't say a thank you. When they arrived home from dropping Sanjay at the airport, Rose did a little happy dance. He tries to muster compassion for Sanjay, to manufacture it because it's not there. Sanjay had two brothers who were successful in ways he wasn't. He had two brothers who shed the bullying, enough so at least, but Sanjay kept carrying it. Sanjay had a grating voice, a bulldozing demeanor that pushed others away. But Vihaan's compassion isn't coming—just disgust, which he feels in his mouth as a thick, oniony rust. Finally, he can taste something but it's not real, and it makes him want to gag. He tries to get rid of the sensation with a vigorous toothbrushing and floss, but it lingers.

He realizes he's spent a lot of time over the course of his life trying to understand what motivates someone to behave sadistically, to understand the psychology of a sociopath. Every time he's heard about senseless violence and dehumanization, the unsolvable puzzles buzz through his thoughts. After the possible school shooter when Doris was teaching, Vihaan went into high alert, imagining that if he could fathom an unfathomable mindset, he'd have a head start against the violence that could leap out and grab him and others by the throat at any moment.

He'd considered Sanjay to be mostly a harmless misfit, but Will's revelation shifted the picture, skewed it. How could someone so closely related to him have lashed out at Will? Had Sanjay been harboring ill will toward Vihaan and only knew how to express it by jabbing Will when the other adults were out of the room?

He has a pain in his jaw and chest. He forces himself to sit upright and chews a couple of antacid tablets, hoping it's just heartburn rather than a heart attack. Then he recalls his own exasperated yelling at Will after Will got the DUI. And, surely, there were dozens of times when he tuned Will out, rolled his eyes at him, didn't give him the common courtesy he'd have given a stranger. He left the nurturing to Rose, sometimes jealous of the attention she lavished on Will, sometimes relieved that he could zone out and watch tennis on television when he wasn't on the court. Will was indifferent to tennis or chess or cooking, and Vihaan didn't know what else to offer him. He'd feign interest in the books or games Will preferred, but Will didn't buy it and talked to Rose or his friends instead. Tonight, Vihaan remembers nodding off during the ponderous plays Will was in during high school, Rose occasionally trying to wake him with a gentle squeeze of his hand, but soon his eyes would be heavy again, and his chin would drift to his chest.

The antacid is doing the trick. He won't die of a heart attack tonight, and thus, he'll have a chance to keep making it up to Will.

The next week's mail brings Vihaan a patent for his biodegradable tennis ball. Doris and Pearl help him figure out how to transfer the patent to Will. In the ensuing months, Will and Darrell, through GoFundMe, have the means to find a manufacturer to make a few hundred prototypes that they send to buyers at Dick's Sporting Goods and Sports Authority. Darrell works as the activities director at an assisted living center where Billie Jean King's cousin lives, and he manages to talk to Billie Jean about the ball. Billie Jean says she'll show the ball to her agent, who knows someone at the International Tennis Federation.

During the Zoom dinners, they talk excitedly about the developments. Barry caters one dinner by having food delivered to Will and Darrell's place from his old restaurant in New York and making an identical meal, with Cliff as his sous chef, at West House. Vihaan's taste buds are starting to revive.

Vihaan ambles in wonky circles around the backyard. He'd been afraid that he'd have nothing to leave Will, no sibling, no mother, no money. He can give Will this ball, this dense sphere, whose biggest virtue is that it will more gracefully and swiftly melt back into the earth, erasing itself instead of persisting as a useless, bald, punctured object that had once bounced and soared and provided entertainment and exercise. He leans against the oak.

He sees himself as the bounceless polluter ball, taking up space when he should make way for the next generation. Maybe that's what Sanjay felt, and for a moment, compassion lights up in Vihaan's thoughts, as bright green as the fuzzy nap on a new tennis ball. But then he doubts that Sanjay was thinking about anyone but himself, and he's afraid that if he keeps trying to generate fellow feeling for his brother, that will detract from his belated defense of Will. He quickly calculates how many hours it will be until the next Zoom dinner.

The backdoor opens, and Doris emerges. Since the pandemic, she hasn't been coloring her hair, and it's grown out white, only reddish at the tips, like an upside-down match. It suits her. She approaches him, holding out a single raisin. "Come to the present," she says.

CHAPTER 25: THE CHALLENGE

ELLEN TELLS JANE about reaching out to her old boyfriend and how he seems to have fallen into the tar pit of dementia. Jane starts thinking about the woman she'd been with when she'd gotten pregnant with Amy, the woman who'd massacred Jane's roses, and she decides to search for Frieda online to see if she has any sort of web presence. That's when she comes upon Frieda's obituary on Legacy.com. She died of a heart attack on November 7, 2016. As deaths go, a nice swift death, the kind Jane wants. Frieda had missed the election and the pandemic. Jane keeps reading. Frieda had become a college dean. She was married to another woman, and they had two children, who are a couple of years younger than Amy, than Amy would have been. Those children have children. Jane closes her computer, not gently as she might on a normal day, but with a loud snap. She feels buzzing in her jaw as if a dentist were drilling there.

She seeks out Barry, who's not home. She settles for Ellen, who agrees to go for a walk with her, and on the sidewalk, Ellen links arms with her, seemingly both to steady her and to slow her down.

"Fuck her," Jane says. "How come when I wanted a child, she couldn't do it, but just a bit later, she was all on board?" She pictures Frieda and her wife rubbing sunscreen on two toddlers at a beach on the cape. A few decades later, they're doing the same thing with their grandchildren.

"You're not going to get answers to your questions. And you can't just fill in the blanks."

Ellen's response sums up something about getting older that chaps Jane. That circumstances have a vast number of variables, many of which might remain undiscovered or unverified, has become more maddening as the years have passed. As she navigates the sidewalk, she's unable, unwilling, to stomp her feet without possibly injuring herself, and that's frustrating too. Still, she can see the humor in wanting to throw a fit and satisfies herself by kicking a pebble down the sidewalk instead.

It does appear that Frieda had the family life Jane had wanted. Maybe, superficially, Ellen does too, but Jane knows enough about Ellen and Tomás not to envy them.

Over tea after one of their noir shows, Jane complains to David, "It's hard to have anything to look forward to these days."

"That's the problem," he says, nodding.

"I know I should be grateful ..."

They hatch a plan, but David says they need to train first. Jane surveys the group to see if anyone would like to train with her, dangling the carrot that will follow the hard work, but they all have excuses not to join in.

David knows a good hill in the neighborhood, just a few blocks from their places. There she takes a few steps gingerly down the steep hill. He hovers nearby, spotting her. She turns around and takes a few steps down. Five steps down, five steps up the first day. Each day she adds three more steps. She feels it in her quads and her glutes.

The last time her body had ached in this satisfying way was after she'd left her vet practice and trained for a marathon. She wanted time away from Amy, who never left the house, and during her runs, Jane could pretend she had nothing to worry about except staying upright, avoiding cars, and drinking in the flora and fauna. As she ran, she sometimes imagined herself lying in the middle of the road, the sweet relief of giving up, lights out. No more responsibility. Amy was strangely protective if Jane ran when it was dark out, nabbing Jane at the doorway and insisting she wear a fluorescent vest and carry a flashlight. Sometimes when out of sight of Amy, she crumpled the vest in her fist and turned off the flashlight. She'd half-hoped that her training for the marathon might inspire Amy to do the hardest thing she could do, but Amy was unreceptive. With the vehemence of a missionary, Amy claimed that the drugs were keeping her alive, an adamant, twisted logic that exhausted Jane. She'd urged Amy to come to Boston for the marathon, to stay with Barry and her at the hotel, but Amy wept and said no cat sitter could do Fred justice. Jane saved her own crying for the last few miles of the marathon, as if the tears were a weight she needed to shed, but she completed it, wanting to prove to herself that she had control over something, despite Amy's precarious existence, despite her own shaking hands.

On the first day that Jane successfully descends the whole hill and climbs back up, David gives a whoop and hugs her.

"I'm so slow," she says.

"Are you in a rush? I'm in no rush. If we weren't out here, I'd be at home procrastinating instead. This feels more fruitful."

She works her way up. One and a fifth hill climbs, one and a quarter, one and a third. She gets to know the skunky smell wafting from the bamboo on the side of the road, sees the overflowing carts out on garbage day, glimpses through a fence a backyard pool and a flash of someone's white flesh bobbing up and down in a butterfly stroke. She gets nervous when an unmasked pedestrian walks past her, breathing near her ear. She's been so trained to look for masks that when she sees people in television commercials who are bare faced, she wonders why they aren't taking precautions. The day she's able to descend and climb the hill twice, her legs tremble and prickle on the way home, and she worries that somehow she's pulled them out of their grooves and she'll have the same kind of tremor in her legs that she's grown to manage in her hands. A warm bath followed by a solid rest in bed from noon to dusk stops her legs from shivering.

Resting in bed, she remembers the year after Amy died, when she'd done online dating and was intrigued by a woman in her sixties who called herself a "bad girl," though the profile didn't explain why. Jane had always tried extra hard to be a good girl, maybe to compensate for her sexual identity, which her parents had insisted was the sinner part of her and which for them dimmed her accomplishments. Then she'd become bad, feeding Amy her drugs for all those years. Jane had stared at the "bad girl's" profile pictures, mesmerized by the way the woman's freckles and age spots blended to give the woman's face a pointillist topcoat. It turned out that what made the woman a bad girl was that during sex, she liked to bite and pinch and slap. These behaviors did nothing to enhance Jane's sexual pleasure, but they satisfied some other need, so Jane's refrain was often "Harder!" After she found herself needing too often to cover up marks the woman left on her and feeling that this masochism caused too much dissonance with her feminism, she found a way to say, "It's not you." She didn't bother trying to retrieve the money she'd loaned the woman for car repairs. She had felt relieved to say goodbye, though she'd missed the part of their relationship that was mundane, like sharing pasta and pesto and watching *Jeopardy*, at which the woman was a whiz. Now she has six people to eat pasta with, to watch *Jeopardy* with, or maybe seven if she counts David. She feels a twinge of guilt, as if she isn't supposed to be upright and cocooned. Then she recalls with a whoosh, a jab in her gut, that none of these people are Amy. Amy is a "was," an irreversible past tense. When Jane had trained for the marathon,

Amy was a weight she tried to shake off by moving, by her body pumping out the distance between them. Though she knows that the reason her body's turned into a piece of dried fruit is age, she feels her juice was first sapped by both Amy's presence and absence.

Jane and David are taking their first out-of-town excursion since the pandemic shutdown. He's packed a picnic and brought along the N95s he had left over from when he'd been using the sander to build shelves. The masks are just in case they need to stop somewhere to use a restroom; they hope to be outside and a good distance from other people otherwise. The disembodied voice on Google Maps guides them down roads that the human to whom the voice belongs has likely never traveled. They are in the Hill Country, and the high wind rocks the unfurling ribbons of trees. While cars zoom past them, David drives the speed limit.

They arrive at Enchanted Rock, a pink granite mountain estimated to be a billion years old, the inside of a volcano that never erupted. At the base, they don their masks briefly for preemptive bathroom visits before they begin. David wears a knapsack filled with picnic fixings and a few bottles of water.

"Bought you a present," David says, opening the pack, fishing around. He hands her a pair of collapsible, lightweight hiking poles.

"How sweet!" she says. "You're too good to me."

It's one foot in front of the other, and it quickly becomes clear that planting the poles is going to be enormous help because the incline is so much steeper than their neighborhood hill. "I read up about the rock," David says. He is behind her, just in case she tumbles backward. The wind is so loud that she has to ask him to speak up. "Right around the rock, they've found arrowheads dating back 11,000 years or so. The rock was also called Crying Rock, maybe because of spirits or just the creaks and groans of nature."

"I like 'Enchanted' better." She'd also read up about the rock, eager to know more about it the same way she'd savor reading a menu online before going to an exciting restaurant. Back in college, when the group would make pilgrimages to the rock about once a year, she didn't have the internet and its wellspring of information at her fingertips. Back then, she just knew that she felt a peace unlike any other when she was atop the mighty rock. "It's 425 feet to the summit," she shares.

Jane stops to admire what looks like a tiny pond for fairies, a sandy-bottomed pool bordered by miniature ferns, an oasis in the middle of a rocky nowhere. She wonders what's in the water that's too small for her naked eye to see. Running a finger under her eyes, she feels the pouches that are always there, a reserve of tears that refuses to lie flat and blend into the rest of her face. She'd like to sit down but is afraid she won't get up again if she does. They have yet to go very far. David smiles at her, encouraging. How different her life would have been if he were the child she'd had. Getting to know him has been the frosting on top of the cake she's found at West House. (She doesn't agree with Barry that good cake doesn't need frosting.)

Other hikers are out, keeping their distance and outpacing them just as the cars did on the road out here. For a bit, Jane counts her steps to assure herself she's making progress. She imagines herself in a sled pulled by a pack of dogs, Mr. Softee and his siblings, only needing to steer. The brisk air has a sugary taste, and she gulps it down. When Amy was little, they'd go into the backyard as it was snowing, each holding a red dessert plate, waiting for it to fill with snow, packing the snow with their bare hands, forming a plate-sized pancake, then dashing back inside to sprinkle the snow with maple syrup and eat it with a spoon. Why hadn't a simple life been enough for Amy?

She has a new floater in her peripheral vision, and it's in the shape of Fred the Cat's tail when he raised it into a question mark.

Maybe she'd been drawn to work with cats and dogs because people are too complicated. On the other hand, the cat that obsessively licks all the fur off its leg, the dog with separation anxiety, the dog that whines when its humans hug each other, surely they have a restless complexity that doesn't afford them ignorant bliss. She feels around in her pocket, finds something as smooth as ashes is in there, and she imagines for a moment that they are Fred's or Amy's. No, just shreds of old tissue.

Jane is standing still, having drifted off. Her breath whistles through her nose. Her legs obey her commands, that miracle, and she keeps hiking.

"When did you first come out here, David?"

"My aunt brought me out here after my parents died."

"I haven't asked you about them yet," she says. "Forgive me."

"We've had other things to talk about. They died in a car crash when I was twelve. Drunk driving. Their own."

"I'm so sorry," Jane says. David has his complexity too, so much of his history that she doesn't know.

"Thank you."

"Did your aunt raise you?"

"She did indeed. She was quite cool. She died a couple of years back, so it's really just me now. So Enchanted Rock seems like a good place for grief to me. I came out here, by the way, after the woman tried to burn down West House. I wanted to get the smoke smell out of my nostrils, the images out of my brain. Like this indestructible rock somehow makes up for fragility."

"I can see that. I'm glad we're friends, David."

His words are like WD-40 on her rusty joints, and her steps become less sluggish. They share a companionable silence as Jane strains to persist, and she's fueled by the recognition that this may be her last time to make such a climb. A chorus sings inside her, "You're alive, you're alive, you're alive." She tells herself that she's done much harder things than climb this mountain. She finds she's holding her breath and has the faintest flash, a panic, of what it might be like to be unable to breathe, whether it's because of COVID or because someone has his knee on your throat. Catching her breath, she blinks and is back in the swirls of sunshine and wind, the privilege of natural wonder, this rock a small planet.

After Jane takes another couple of dozen arduous steps, David asks, "Would you like to stop here?"

"Hell no!"

"Understood."

Jane pauses, does a slow 360, taking in the views from all angles. Brown strata dotted with broccoli trees, the mackerel sky. Then onward, Jane's legs protesting but her will saying yes, until they reach the top.

"We did it, we did it!" sings David, doing a little jig.

She admires his delight. They find a cluster of rocks that are wide enough for seating. He produces the food from his pack, bagels and lox with thick smears of cream cheese, and he hands Jane a large bottle of water. Jane waits until her breath slows and she's had a few chugs of water to take her first bite, the saltiness of the lox and the chewiness of the bagel just right for replenishment.

On one occasion when Jane had come to Enchanted Rock as a college student, she'd been with Barry. They'd recently come out of the closet to each other, and Barry was free to discuss in great detail his lust for Tomás. Jane had shared her first kiss with a lithe Lady Longhorn basketball player, and she savored the memory, the woman's lips and tongue as soft as raspberries, as she and Barry had made the climb, their young legs cooperating without a twinge.

After lunch, Jane and David meander to a facet of the rock that has a sheer drop. As they stand there, Jane thinks about what it would be like to leap over the edge, her arms flapping like wings. She'd go while the going was good, on a lovely day, with the clean air filtering out the insidious virus. No more worries. The end of grief. But if she left now, she wouldn't have completed the hike for which she'd trained. She'd be cheating. Plus, she couldn't do that to David. Instead, she reaches out and takes David's hand, anchoring herself. He adds his other hand to their clasp so her hand is safely sandwiched between his.

The hike down is slow and wobbly. David offers to take Jane in the firefighter's carry, and for the second time today, she says, "Hell no." The words feel liberating, as bracing as Barton Springs was on the day she'd gone swimming with Byron. Midway down, her legs crumple, and David catches her before she hits the ground. She steadies, plants each foot firmly, toe to heel. Nimble climbers, one in a magenta hoodie, another in a fluorescent green jacket, on their journeys up and down, pass by waving and wishing them a good afternoon. Maybe some of them are nursing crushes, remembering raspberry kisses.

Jane falls asleep on the car ride home. Over the weeks that follow, she keeps practicing her climbs up and down the nearby hill, and sometimes instead of boring gray concrete under her feet, she sees eternal pink granite.

Chapter 26: Dependency

CLIFF RUNS HIS stubbly chin over Barry's back. When he digs his chin in and scrapes it over the skin, Barry feels a burn, and when Cliff just skates his chin over the surface, Barry feels a tickle. He regrets the years he and Cliff didn't know each other and the months of their separation that now seem pointless. Or maybe the point was for them to appreciate each other more.

It's February, and tomorrow's Valentine's Day. For the past few days, the news has been of a winter storm watch and concerns about the power grid. Rolling blackouts are a possibility. The grocery store shelves sit forlorn, mostly empty of water and staples, but Cliff is a planner and has a pantry full of supplies, enough to help out West House if needed.

Barry's not particularly worried because they've had Snowpocalypse warnings in Austin before, and the snow has been barely enough to make a snow cone, let alone a snowperson. He remembers that first romantic evening at Cliff's, during the freezing rain, when they took a bath together for the first time, saw each other's sags and creases as well as the parts of them that were still vibrant and elastic. Barry suggests a bath now, and Cliff is game. Cliff mixes a cup of lavender bath salts into the steaming water. They try to make love in the tub, but that requires painful contortions, so they give up, settling for earnest kissing.

Barry and Cliff have planned a staycation at Cliff's, just the two of them. Taking long walks, cooking and baking, napping, playing chess and cribbage are on the agenda. As the temperature drops, they wrap Cliff's outside faucets and lay sheets over the prickly pears and aloe. Sitting on the sofa, his argyle-socked feet propped on the coffee table, Cliff raises his head from Barry's shoulder and says, "It's been so long since I've skated." There was no news about when the skating rink might reopen. "What if I've lost it?" He looks dejected. It's that look that Jane had the day after she came back from Enchanted Rock; her elation at making it up and down the rock was overshadowed by pangs about the possibility of never doing it again.

"We'll get our vaccines soon, wait a couple of weeks. By then, the rink has got to be open."

Cliff says, "I never used to worry about falling and breaking something, but now that crosses my mind. I'm rusty, maybe too old."

"But think of all the years you put in. Surely, the ability doesn't die that quickly." Still, it had been almost a year now. They'd last skated the Friday in mid-March when the schools had snapped shut. Though Barry had strengthened his arms these past months during his pull-up attempts, he knew his leg muscles could use work, and his general skating chops were nowhere near as well developed as Cliff's. He should be the one worried about breaking his kneecap or coccyx at the rink, but the thought of a non-fatal accident didn't cow him the way it might have pre-pandemic. The magnitude of bad news had ballooned this year, as if in the new normal, every bathroom scale now had the ability to handle a ton.

They're in the middle of their Valentine's meal when they get a call. The power has gone out at West House. The news now is that the blackouts aren't rolling but indefinite. Jane's going to stay with David, who still has a generator so she can keep an eye on the semi-feral cats. David will help her bring the outdoor heated cat houses to his backyard where they can be plugged into live outlets.

The rest of the group, they decide, will come to Cliff's house and stay in his guest room and his Airbnb unit with its queen bed and sofa bed. "You're such a good egg," Barry says to Cliff after Cliff makes the offer and starts gathering towels to distribute. Though he'd like to think he would be, Barry doesn't know if he'd be as open armed if five of Cliff's friends showed up for open-ended food and shelter.

As he's thinking this, Cliff's doorbell rings. It's the man from next door, Albert, who is a frail-looking, bent-over ninety-something year old. His terrier, Maeve, in a coat the bright orange of traffic cones, is at his ankles. "I'm not sick. Haven't been around anybody," he announces. His power's out too, so Cliff makes him a cup of tea. After urgent whispers in Cliff's bedroom, Barry and he decide that the living room couch will be adequate for Albert and Maeve, and they don't have to relinquish their bed. They exchange a look of guilt and relief. Cliff heads to Albert's house to fetch Albert's medicine and a bed and food for Maeve, while Barry stands shivering on the front porch. The Odyssey turns onto the icy street, progressing at a crawl. It slides across its lane, but luckily no one is coming from the other direction. With a shudder and a gasp, it settles in Cliff's driveway.

Barry thinks how young his housemates look next to Albert as they sit in the living room and finish off the apple olive oil cake that Barry had made at Cliff's request. Tomás catches Barry's eye, and Barry thinks of raising his wine glass to him, but maybe that would be perceived as rubbing it in to Tomás who's still sober. Vihaan, Doris, and Pearl will stay in the back house. Vihaan thinks it will be healing to him to stay there now that he's well instead of struggling with COVID. "And with good company," he says, putting one arm around Doris and one around Pearl.

Pearl and Ellen are sandwiching Albert on the sofa that will be become his bed, and when they notice that he's dozed off, the West housemates, minus Barry, creep up and make their ways to the rooms where they'll be sleeping. Cliff covers Albert with a quilt and slips off his shoes, Albert mumbling but not fully waking. They leave the kitchen light on so Albert won't awake to disorienting darkness—that is, if the power stays on.

Barry has trouble sleeping and wanders to the kitchen to get a glass of water. Albert is now tipped over on the sofa, seemingly completely still, so Barry sidles up to him and lays a hand on his side to find that indeed it still rises and falls. He remembers staying with Jane after Amy died; she left her bedroom door open, and he'd sneak in to see that she was indeed both asleep and alive, not quite trusting her to rest or to stay tethered to this world.

Maeve whimpers from her bed, unfolds onto stiff legs, and follows Barry back to the bedroom, where he scoops her up and lets her lie next to him, her rapid breathing like a staccato metronome. It's wise of her to cuddle up to strangers because surely she might outlast Albert. Barry feels both irritated and guilty when he awakes to Albert's plaintive voice calling Maeve. It's three in the morning, the wind howling, as Barry returns the dog to the living room. Albert looks at him suspiciously, as if he'd been holding Maeve against her will. "She's a good girl," Barry says, and Albert looks softened by the admiration. Barry thinks of an exhibit of photos he'd seen of people before and after they'd been told they were beautiful, the after photos so full of light.

Barry can see through the living room window that the snow is higher than he's ever seen in Austin. According to the thermostat, it's 15 degrees outside. He wonders where Ruby is right now. All around the state, pandemic-weary people are undergoing this fresh hit, in some cases choosing to risk the virus by huddling together in the dark to offset the cold and in other cases braving it alone but risking freezing.

Barry starts when Albert asks, "Are you Cliff's brother?" He'd thought Albert had dozed off again.

"I'm his boyfriend," Barry says.

"Boyfriend ..." Albert mutters. "Hmm." He hides his head under the blanket, and Barry returns to Cliff's side. Barry can already anticipate how this restless night will cause him to drag through the day. He's both jealous and admiring of Cliff's ability to sail off into uninterrupted slumber, Cliff, like Albert, as still as can be.

The group saves Barry a couple of pancakes, and Maeve jumps onto his lap as he eats, surreptitiously handing her pieces of the pancake that he's sliced like a pie. Though his gut doesn't like it, he gulps two piping hot espressos to get more perky. He receives a text from the city of Austin alerting citizens about an advisory to boil water before drinking it or using it for toothbrushing. They can still shower. He shares the news with the group, and a chorus of boos swells. The chorus crescendos, frustration unleashed.

Vihaan stands. "Enough!" he says. "No griping! Complain, complain. We're damn lucky to all be alive. Can't we just be grateful?"

The group looks sobered. Barry remembers how worried he was when Vihaan was in the back house, shivering and sweating through the virus. What would he have done if he'd delivered a meal and Vihaan never took it inside? What if they'd been unable to get in touch with him?

"Water comes out of our taps," Vihaan says. "It's a luxury. Just think about Pearl and Flint. Think about people without electricity whose electric stoves won't boil water."

Pearl nods vigorously.

"My stove is gas," Cliff volunteers for those not already in the know. "And I've got a bunch of bottled drinks, including water. Plus there's the fireplace." The living room fireplace is stacked with Duraflame logs.

Tomás starts into "For He's a Jolly Good Fellow," and the others join, Albert surprising Barry with the vigorousness of his voice. Maeve whines along.

"Would you like me to take her for a walk?" Barry asks Albert.

Though he doesn't meet Barry's eye, Albert nods yes. Cliff has grippy hiking boots that fit Barry, so he laces them up. Ellen wants to join him, and she dons one of those puffer jackets that can be squished into a small pouch. They are tentative in the snow, unsure of what's underneath it, Maeve prancing forward a few steps, then slinking back.

"Here we are, dependent on you again. On your connections, your largesse," Ellen says with a smile but an edgy tone.

"Wow," he says. "What's this about?"

"What if you get tired of us and move in with Cliff? Where will we be?"

"Y'all are my family," he says. "I've been lucky when it comes to money, and I can share that with all of you. That's what it says in my will, and that's my plan, living or dead. You six are my main family now that the rest of it is gone." His older siblings are no longer alive.

"Oh, Barry, why didn't you tell us? I knew you had our backs, but not to that extent." She packs a light snowball and throws it at his arm; it falls apart midair.

"It seems gross to talk about money, to feel like you'll think you have to suck up to me, or I'll cut you out of the will." Maybe money, like death, is such an uncomfortable topic that it's seemed unnecessary to go there. Maybe he'd just rather focus on the next meal, the next day, and whether he can get closer to a chin-up.

Maybe he needs to stop playing games and get each roommate a copy of his will.

Maeve has chosen this moment to make a poo that seems out of proportion to her small body.

"To be honest, since you're the landlord, I've felt like I had to be extra-nice to you. Not that I don't love you to pieces," she says. "Don't you remember what it's like to worry about money?"

He nods. Though it's so distant now, he knows he could barely stay awake in school because he hadn't had enough to eat, and his body was running on empty, gnawing on itself. His hand-me-down pants had been baggy and stained, barely held up by a belt of frayed rope.

"I'm afraid Tomás and I will outlive our money, and you'll have to put us on an ice floe and bid us adieu."

He hugs her, feels her bones beneath the vibrant, artificial puff of her jacket. "Freaky weather aside, I doubt that we're going to be able to find an ice floe anywhere." He bags up Maeve's waste, and they head back to the house.

It's eerily silent. Something's missing from the regular nature soundtrack, and he realizes that the mourning doves, whom he hears whenever he's outside, are taking a break. Maybe they're too cold or tired to sing. Maybe they're all huddled together for warmth. He hopes Ruby has found shelter.

Inside, the friends are playing charades. From Pearl's mugging, Barry guesses that she's acting out *Titanic*, but he's not on a team and doesn't wait to find out whether his guess is correct before he excuses himself to take a nap. He falls into a deep sleep despite the waves of laughter outside the bedroom.

When he awakens, it's dark, and it takes a while to orient himself. He forces himself up and to the kitchen, where a few of the group are seated eating cheese and crackers and drinking wine. Albert is alone in the living room, with Maeve on his lap, staring off into space. He's becoming part of the couch.

"You all right there?" Barry asks.

"Splendid," says Albert, though Barry doesn't know how to read him. Albert has still not met his gaze since Barry revealed the nature of his relationship with Cliff.

Barry goes back to the kitchen and pronounces "I'll cook" to enthusiastic response. He contemplates making what he craves, a fiery Indian chickpea dish. He goes as far as to check that Cliff has the ingredients, which he does, but then decides that putting something milder in front of Albert might be fairer. Albert is, after all, at their mercy, the odd man out, sleeping on a couch that looks better than it feels.

Barry returns to the living room and asks, "Do you like chicken and dumplings?"

Though no one else is in the room, Albert says, "Are you asking me?"

"Yes, sir."

Maybe the "sir" is the on switch because now Albert is finally looking at him or toward him. "Do I. Can't remember the last time I had 'em though."

It occurs to Barry, at this delayed point, that Albert might not see very well. "Right, then. Should be ready in an hour."

At dinner, Cliff asks Vihaan, "How is it to stay in that bed where you … where you …"

"Struggled? Thought I might die? It's a luxury. Thank you."

"Die of what?" Albert asks.

Vihaan fills him in.

"And look at you now," Albert says. "Welcome back to the world."

Barry wonders whom Albert has lost. You can't get to be his age without a boatload of your people leaving the world. Then there are other losses. The loss of ability to spring up from a couch or to easily retrieve something that's fallen to the floor. Albert's wearing scuffed slip-on loafers. At some point, he might have lost the option of wearing lace-up shoes. And how does he clean the floor of his shower? Maybe Maeve keeps him in shape. He has to bend over to clean up after her on their walks, or maybe he just lets her go in the yard, where he doesn't have to bother. Barry tries to imagine the erosion of his abilities and wonders if he'll see himself losing abilities from one day to the next or whether he'll just realize he can't do something anymore but won't remember when he last could.

The lights flicker out, and Cliff says, "Uh oh." The streetlights blink out too, and the only light remaining is moonlight, faint strands of it through the frost-laced windows. Cliff has a few rechargeable flashlights plugged in around the front and back houses, so they're able to use those to settle into the long night. Cliff insists that Albert wear his down coat, wool cap, and Thinsulate gloves. He puts a second pair of socks on Albert's thin feet. Pearl is the only one besides Albert not sharing a bed, so Ellen gives her the puffer coat.

Barry snaps awake at 3 a.m. again, as if from an alarm. He ventures into the living room to see if Albert is alive and finds him standing next to a potted plant in the corner of the living room. He hears liquid hissing into the soil. He retreats before Albert can turn around and notice him. Not even Maeve seems to be aware of his presence.

Though unwashed and poorly slept, they survive the next couple of days before they're able to say "Let there be light" as they flip a switch at Cliff's place, West House, and Albert's house. Still, big swathes of rosemary and prickly pear in their yards are dead, as if the plants were unfortunate houses chosen by a selective tornado.

In April, Albert's niece, who was up the impassable interstate highway during the freeze, lets Cliff know that Albert has died of pneumonia. He was diagnosed at urgent care, but with no hospital beds open nearby, Albert insisted that he was all right at home.

Barry feels a pang, as if he and Cliff should have followed up with Albert more after he returned home, as if he and Cliff should have grown fonder of him. Occasionally, Barry imagines Albert drowning, which he figures dying of pneumonia must be like. His throat tightens, and he has to remind himself to exhale.

After West House votes Maeve in, at the urging of Barry, Jane, and Cliff, Barry makes the adoption offer to the niece, who accepts, relieved. "Uncle Cliff is here," Cliff announces when he comes over and scoops up the little dog, who never seems to tire of all the attention.

Barry doesn't mention to anyone how Albert watered Cliff's plant, which seems none the worse for it.

Chapter 27: Control

GREGORY PECK IS the cashier at Target; there's a long line, and he apologizes to Pearl when it's finally her turn to check out. "Oh, no, I don't mind waiting at all," she says. Then she's hanging out in his living room with his friends, hoping they'll leave, so she and Gregory can go to bed together. That doesn't happen before she wakes up, alone, but she's smiling nonetheless.

The library has reopened, and she keeps wondering if Ruby will appear. One day she even takes a furtive sniff of the chair in which Ruby used to settle. No hint of her. She calls the central library and learns Ruby hasn't been there either. But here's the man who harassed Ruby. Couldn't he have been placed on a no-entry list? But they have no such list. She has to ask him to wear a mask, and he grumbles about it but puts one on, resting it below his nose. "All the way up," she says. With someone else, she would have used a "please." He gives her the evil eye but acquiesces. She looks away and plucks stray hairs from her shirt.

She's glad to have the job again because it forces her to walk more, and, as if her brain had become a dull pencil, it seems sharper again. She'd felt great relief when Barry called a group meeting and explained to them that he had their backs financially, beyond just the prorated rent. Still, she likes the stimulation at the library of being around kids and younger people. David is the baby among their friend group, and he just turned fifty, so for over a year, she'd not kept company with youngsters.

Lately, she's been shedding a lot. After she showers, she combs her hair and is dismayed by how much hair she has to clean from the comb. Her thick braid has been her signature look, and she figured she was wed to it until death. But her hair has a plan of its own. She asks her doctor about it, and the doctor does a thyroid test, which comes back in the normal range. Her braid grows thinner, wispier.

She finds herself at Ellen's hair stylist, still masked, but her head dipped back in a flow of warm water, while the stylist massages her shoulders and neck and finally uses shampoo and conditioner that smell like honeysuckle.

"You're a bit tense, darling," the stylist says. "Your neck."

She nods. "And my hair's been falling out."

"I've been seeing that a lot lately. People all stressed by the pandemic. Hair knows."

When the stylist finishes, Pearl opting for a pixie cut a bit like Ellen's, Pearl looks in the mirror and sees her father. She's no longer the aged hippie chick but a no-nonsense person with a fine set of cheekbones and artfully tousled, thicker-looking hair. The stylist gives Pearl the braid in a plastic Ziploc, and Pearl stashes it in her purse as if it were a snack or good luck talisman.

The next morning in the shower, she's shocked by how little hair she has left to shampoo. When she runs her hand over her head, her hair ends abruptly. She enjoys the novelty of her reflection in the mirror, the unfamiliar shape of herself.

At the library, the obnoxious man is back with his mask dangling below his mouth.

"Mask needs to be all the way up, covering your mouth and nose."

He flips it back up and moves closer to her. He then pulls it down, like a flasher, and proceeds to cough in her face, a mist of saliva, a deep bark. For a moment, she's frozen. Then she pivots on her heel and retreats behind the front desk. With a tissue, she rubs her cheeks and her lips, trying to rid herself of the man's germs. Meanwhile, the man has disappeared. Nonetheless, a coworker gives her a ride home after work because she feels trepidation about walking by herself.

She takes off the next few days, monitoring each twinge, each moment of scratchiness in her throat, for hints of having contracted the virus. She pictures herself slashing the obnoxious man's tires, doesn't like the desire for vengeance that rises in her throat like vomit. Although the roommates don't think she needs to quarantine, she eats at different times than they do and spends a great amount of time in her room playing solitaire and phoning the siblings with whom she'd been in scant contact. When she tells her sister that she's cut her hair, her sister cries out, like Jo's younger sister in *Little Women*, "Your hair! Your one beauty."

Before exiting the bathroom, she disinfects the surfaces. Maeve scratches on her bedroom door, and she lets her in, grateful to touch a living being.

The man doesn't return to her branch of the library, but she talks to an acquaintance at another branch, and he's been there. He may be making his unwelcome way around the city, visiting the sanctuaries, spewing pollution like a factory, blasting noise like an engine whose byproduct is to disturb, to wake up the neighbors.

One late afternoon on her walk home, Pearl sees the man get out of his pickup truck and enter a dark bar. She stands still, out of sight, wondering what to do. She approaches the truck, tries a door, but it's locked. The cover to the gas cap opens by pressing on it, and she unscrews the cap. She fetches her braid from her purse and fishes it out of its plastic bag. She stuffs the braid through the door to the fuel tank, feeling it unravel as she does so, imagining the hair disintegrating in the caustic fuel.

When she trots away, lighter, she feels as if she's made a statement. But by the time she reaches West House, she halts outside the front door, seeing that her gesture was hollow, and shame suffuses her like a hot flash. A red-headed woodpecker taps away at a nearby tree, seeking food, shelter, a mate, territory, who knows? Still, she drinks it in with her eyes and her ears, all the world falling away and shrinking to this driven bird, this patient tree. She doesn't mind waiting as the sun sets, until she's jarred by the front door opening, by Barry beckoning her into the light-filled house.

Chapter 28: Continuum of Care

TOMÁS WAKES HER up as he trips over some of the piled-up supplies that are creeping from his side of the room to hers. The room seems to be shrinking as he continues to accumulate more art supplies. "But I might use this," he says as he adds to the piles. Ellen has shrunk a bit herself lately, lost ten pounds over the course of this ongoing pandemic, as if his hogging up space forces her to inhabit less of it. She hasn't been conscious of cutting back her food intake and has a niggling worry that the weight loss is a sign of the return of her cancer; she hopes no one notices because she doesn't want to explore it, whatever its source. Also niggling are the unpaid medical bills she accumulated over the course of her treatment—deductibles and copays, they add up. It's easier to slip the bills into a drawer than figure out from where the money could come.

She and Tomás have been invited to visit old friends who've moved recently from Dallas to Austin and are living in a spiffy continuum-of-care facility that looks like a resort from the pictures on the website over which Ellen has lingered. For 700K down and 15K a month, one could rent an apartment, and when still-older age and disease make it difficult to shower or eat or dress oneself, one could move to the next higher level of care without a penalty; same for even higher levels of care, and if one ran out of money, for a good reason, the place would float you.

Such a lovely safety net would have required foresight and earning power Ellen and Tomás had never had. She reminds herself that Barry is their continuum of care, though that idea still feels wobbly. She's been tempted to sneak into his room when he's at Cliff's and look at his files, try to determine by riffling through his papers how much he's really got, as if a number could reassure her, the number like a reassuring hotline for help. She hasn't seen any statements addressed to him when she's fetched the mail and realizes the information she'd like to see is probably password protected.

Ever since they received the invitation to visit their friends at Pecan Place, Ellen has thought of the husband of the couple, Jay, and how maybe ten or fifteen years from now, after both of their spouses have died not too painful deaths, she and Jay might get together. Then they'd move into a different apartment at Pecan Place so his and his wife's memories wouldn't be in flakes of dead skin embedded in the carpet, and she'd be able to relax more profoundly, be able to swim every day in the pool pictured on the website, to never do a dish again because three meals were provided. She likes the idea that life could still surprise her with a second marriage, both fresh and secure.

They dress up for the dinner, Tomás in a turquoise linen guayabera and flattering black trousers, she in a gray satin sheath and strappy sandals, sparkly earrings. Ellen notices that the front of her dress drapes awkwardly over the flat part of her chest, but Tomás assures her that she looks lovely. She reciprocates. They have fresh black KN95s for the areas of Pecan Place that require them.

Jay and Janet's apartment, where they have an aperitif and Tomás a club soda, has high ceilings and floor-to-ceiling windows in the living room. They have a view of downtown, including the building that looks like a giant tweezers sparkling silver as the sun sets in candy pinks and apricot. On one wall, the couple has an enormous family portrait, their kids looking sporty, the parents so young, and Ellen finds herself being drawn to look at it, a wave of regret washing over her that she and the family didn't take more pictures. She'd always so disliked herself in them that she'd shied away. Also, her distance from Tomás and the kids had made her feel as if she hadn't a right to possess their images, that to do so would make her vampiric.

Jay is staring at her as Janet catches them up on their kids, all of whom live in Austin. His gaze sweeps over her neatly crossed legs, and she enjoys the sense of power. The air conditioning blows on the back of her neck, goose-pimples her bare arms. Tomás takes her hand as he recounts their children's and grandchildren's news for Jay and Janet. He mentions a recent accomplishment Luz had of which Ellen had been unaware. She feels that queasiness she'd felt when she'd neglected to note the exact location of her car in a parking lot and had to search for it; on at least one occasion, she'd set off the car alarm on her key fob so she could find it. She's grateful that these days, someone else is always driving, and she can depend on the driver to be the guardian of the parking spot.

The Pecan Place dining room has numerous chandeliers, white tablecloths, black napkins, weighty silverware and glasses. The diners are white, Tomás having the brownest face except for the masked servers, who are mostly people of color with a few older white people who look like they could have benefited from retirement too, but instead are spending the evening blending into the background of the more fortunate. The two couples don their reading glasses to peruse tonight's menu. Ellen wonders why it's not in large print. Perhaps that would be an unwanted admission of the need, or perhaps the menu would then be an unwieldy several pages.

Ellen has always liked Janet and has a qualm about killing her off in her idle fantasy of her future with Jay. Back before Jay and

Janet had a lot of money, Ellen liked the way Janet hadn't seemed to care about whether her house or her hair was clean; she liked that at the local pool, Janet had hairy armpits and muscular calves and could do a flip off the diving board. After Jay and Janet acquired more money and after rumors from mutual friends that Jay had almost left Janet for his colleague, Janet's house and appearance became more constricted, a sort of camouflage.

Janet reaches for a warm roll from the basket that was placed on the table shortly after they sat down. Jay shoots a look at her, and she tears off a tiny piece of the roll before placing the rest of it on Jay's bread plate. Tomás takes a roll, tears off a tiny piece of it, and places the rest of it on Janet's bread plate, then does the same for Ellen. Jay glares at Tomás and proceeds to tell them at length about the vintage of the bottle of wine he's brought to the table. When he tries to pour Tomás a glass, Tomás politely refuses.

"I remember you being able to tuck it away. Many a time," Jay says.

"That was ages ago," Tomás says. "It doesn't agree with me now. But thank you."

"More for the rest of us," Jay says.

A pianist comes in and starts to play "Smoke Gets in Your Eyes."

"They play music from the time when our short-term memory was good," Janet says.

"Are you okay?" Ellen asks. With a real possibility of Janet suffering, she grows uneasy.

"Good enough," Janet says and pats Ellen's hand. "Sometimes I forget people's names but just call them 'darling.'"

They hear a scuffle and a cry, "He's choking!" from across the dining room. A server races out from behind a row of potted plants to perform the Heimlich. As this happens, the room seems to have collectively inhaled; the pianist stops mid-song. At last, the raw bark of a cleared pathway. "I'm fine," shouts the choker. "At ease!" Conversations resume, and the pianist plays the rest of "My Girl."

Under the table, someone's foot brushes Ellen's, and she's determined not to look but just tucks her feet under her chair. Janet's hand trembles as she holds her wine glass, and a drop of red escapes to color the tablecloth. Her sleeve brushes the brown crust of her filet mignon, which leaves a stain. Ellen's also having a filet mignon since that's something they don't have at home. For a moment, she visualizes the cow from which it came, those enormous brown eyes, expressive like Janet's. Now Ellen's no longer hungry.

"Excuse me," she says, standing up.

"I'll show you the way," Jay offers, and Ellen plasters on a smile.

It's indeed a bit of a labyrinth to find the restroom, and Ellen wonders about the utility of this arrangement with a bunch of seniors.

Outside the women's room, Jay says, "I'll wait for you."

"Oh, no need. I have a good sense of direction."

"No trouble."

As she's sitting on the toilet, someone else enters the restroom. She hurries to finish up and opens the stall door to see Jay standing there.

"What are you doing?" she asks.

"You're looking kind of fluffy," Jay says. Ellen realizes that the last time he saw her, she was probably 98 pounds, and she's 20 pounds heavier now. "Like a dessert."

"Don't be ridiculous."

She tries to shoulder past him, to get out the door. He grasps her arms, holding her in place, his bloodshot eyes contrasting with his slick smile. He lets go of one of her arms and runs his hand over the breast that didn't have surgery, then over the one that did. Ellen's cancer hadn't come up in their conversation. He lurches back, waving his hand as if it were burnt. She takes that hand and bends his pinky back, and he grimaces with contemptuous anger, the way Brett Kavanaugh did when confronted by his accuser during the hearings from which Ellen hadn't been able to tear herself away. She lets go and dashes out the door.

She arrives back at the table before Jay. Holding Janet's hand, she says, "I'm so sorry, but I have a splitting headache. I think we should go. Thanks so much for the dinner."

"Oh, you have to wait for Jay to say goodbye."

Ellen counts to sixty in her head. "Please just tell Jay good night from us."

Janet hugs each of them tightly. Ellen notices a card key on Jay's chair and palms it as they stand to leave.

Earlier, when Jay and Janet had given the tour, they'd stopped by the atrium where the pool and hot tub are. Now Ellen leads Tomás there, and he says, "What the hell?" when she unveils the key.

"We really shouldn't. I thought you had a headache," Tomas says, following her in, unbuttoning his shirt.

"I don't. Jay was inappropriate."

"That prick!"

"I bent back his pinky."

"Good job. Are you okay?"

"Yes, and there's no one here but us," she says. "We'll never be back here again."

He has on an undershirt, which he hands her because she has no bra. In their underwear, they sink into the hot tub, hold hands under the water. The chlorine bleaches out Jay's touch. Ellen's eyes grow hot with grief or relief or gratitude, or maybe all three. They play around in the pool, swimming through each other's legs, carrying each other's lighter bodies. When they're ready to go home, they "borrow" one of the stacked sumptuous towels, monogrammed "PP," from a cubby and wrap up the wet underwear. Ellen tosses the card key into the pool, and it pinwheels in slow motion, reminding her of the floating sock in the sinkhole. As they walk to the parking lot, it's warmer outdoors than it was inside, and she likes the feel of the breeze on her arms and legs. She takes Tomás's old familiar arm and hugs it close to her side.

The next day she draws Janet, with silver hair on her head and under her arms, in a violet bathing suit, doing a swan dive into a pale green pool. She takes a photo of it, attaches it to an email to Janet with a brief note, "To your spirit. Thanks again! XO Ellen."

Janet expresses her delight in a return email and writes, "Are you feeling better today?"

"Much," writes Ellen.

Tomás acquires boxes for his art supplies that he can fit under the bed and makes the room less crowded, quieter.

Chapter 29: Encore

IT'S AFTER MIDNIGHT when Doris goes for a glass of water. In the kitchen, she sets down her glass and notices that the counter is warm. Next to the counter, a burner on the stove is still on, its thin neon blue ring of fire barely detectable, but still there. It's unlikely that anything catastrophic could happen from the neglect, but she's uneasy, wondering who did it, why no one else has noticed it, remembering how her parents leaving on the stove burners could be read as early signs of their dementia. When they entered the memory care unit, after she could no longer both work and take care of them, she felt relief that they hadn't killed anyone by absentmindedness at home or by their erratic driving in their big boat of a Lincoln.

At breakfast, which she's cooked as her daily chore, Doris mentions the lit burner, but no one steps forward as the last one yesterday to use the stove. Vihaan wants to go on a walk with her, but she asks to walk by herself; he looks a bit deflated and waves to her as if she were leaving for a long journey. A few blocks from West House, another sinkhole is being repaired. The repair vehicles make those maddening backing-up beeps, and she hurries to find a quieter place.

As she walks, she remembers the drive from Los Angeles back to San Diego to see what was left of her house after the fire. She went with the wife of the couple with whom she'd been staying. When they entered the neighborhood, it smelled of burnt plastic, burnt hair. The whole block had blurred into a stagnant sea of ashes; at what seemed to be the site of the house, the friend took a Ziploc bag out of her purse and scooped up a handful of the ashes to give to Doris. Doris's knees had felt tenuous, and she'd imagined lying on the ground and making an ash angel, trying to force beauty into the wreckage. Her home was underinsured, irreplaceable, and her L.A. friend offered her low rent on a tiny casita they had. That's where she lived until returning to Austin.

Today, she's missing her husband, Howard. She'd loved the way he ran his hand through her hair, how he quietly tithed to causes he and she chose each year, how he struck up conversations with strangers. He liked to entertain; he cooked, and she cleaned up. Before him, her social life was the occasional meal or movie with female friends and the Saturday folk dancing. After they got together, she saw his delight in fitting together numerous outings and hosting dinners as if each occasion were a piece in a jigsaw puzzle of Impressionist art.

She wants to run away. If she stays, she and her friends will end up taking care of each other in more profound and exhausting ways, and she doesn't want that burden. She's especially feeling the weight of her attachment to Vihaan, the sickness-and-health principle that their bond implies even though they're not formally married.

She tries to stomp the dust off her red Chuck Taylors to no avail. A bus is idling at the corner, and she pulls on her mask as she approaches. She asks the bus driver if he can break a twenty or if she can use a credit card, but he just laughs and waves her on. She texts Vihaan, "Decided to make a day of my walk. See you later!" Heart emoji.

"Enjoy," he replies with no punctuation. She doesn't know how to read his tone.

The windows of the bus are open, and a relieving breeze circulates. She pictures her mother's empty look, the lack of recognition; she remembers lying to her mother about her father's death because she didn't want to keep breaking the news to her. "Oh, Mr. Bennett is working," she'd say because her mother couldn't distinguish her from the other strangers who came to her room, and her mother seemed satisfied with the answer until she asked again another five minutes later. "We're supposed to go dancing," her mother once announced. "My husband and me. I'll introduce you."

"Oh, that's exciting! What will you wear?"

"To what, dear?"

That might have been the last time her mother spoke to her. After that, if she was awake, she seemed frustrated that no one was speaking a language she understood. She'd squeezed her eyes shut and waved her hands as if shooing away gnats.

"Last stop," the bus driver calls.

The block of the bus stop has a piñata store, in the window of which is a giant piñata of Trump wearing a diaper. Doris passes a pawnshop, a gas station, a tiny storefront advertising "Pollo Al Carbon." After a bit, she turns into a residential neighborhood with no sidewalks. Most of the houses have bars on the windows. On the patchy front lawn of one, a girl of about eight sits at a card table on which are a plastic jug with neon yellow liquid and red Solo cups. The girl has a fountain of curly black hair and wears a pale blue shorts set with a matching mask. "Lemonade, lady. Dollar fifty. Comes with a dance, and you get to sit in my chair."

"Sounds like a good deal. How come you're not in class?"

"The homework was to create a business."

This seems ill advised for the child's age range and during a pandemic, but Doris accepts the explanation. "Change for a twenty?" she asks.

The girl scribbles something on a piece of paper and announces, "Eighteen-fifty. Unless you want to leave a tip."

"Of course. Make it eighteen."

"Watch the booth," the girl says as she disappears inside her house.

She sits in the girl's chair, which is child-sized. In a minute, the girl skips out of the door, followed by an older woman wearing a white bucket hat. The woman says, "Doris! Is that you?"

It takes Doris a moment to recognize Maria, a fellow folk dancer, but they grin, bump elbows, the acceptable way to touch these days. Maria says, "This is my granddaughter, Serena." Serena wiggles as she pours Doris a cup of lemonade, which is so sweet-sour that it makes her thirstier, but she'll wait a bit to ask for a water chaser.

"Serena, give us a few minutes to catch up. You can cue up the music, and maybe bring us some water and melon too."

"Should I charge extra for that?" Serena stage-whispers to her grandmother.

Maria stage-whispers back. "No, this is special for people we know and like."

"Ach, *abuela*. You like too many people."

Serena skips off again, and while she's gone, Doris and Maria quickly fill each other in on how they've been and whether they've lost anyone close to them (Maria's sister is gone). It flicks through Doris's mind that Ruby might also be gone; Pearl's been talking about that possibility. Doris and Maria keep their hands to themselves, sit six feet or so apart, but in normal times, Doris would have grabbed Maria's hand by this point, would have leaned in closer to show her care. Each of them still wears a mask, so Doris can't see if Maria is wearing the carnation pink lipstick she wore to the dances.

When Serena returns, she finds a tune on her phone for the promised dance. It's got a catchy beat, Maria and Doris clap to it, and soon Serena is scrambling on the ground in break-dance moves, followed by doing the worm, and throwing in a flip at the last moment. The adults give her a standing ovation.

"Encore!" Doris cries.

"What's that mean?"

"Again!"

Serena looks questioningly at Maria, and Maria nods. Serena starts another song, outdoing herself with a compelling frenzy. At the end of the song, she flops onto the lawn and rolls around like an animal taking a dirt bath, which Maria doesn't try to interrupt. Doris feels a swell of envy and admiration—of Serena, of Maria. After Serena jumps up and brushes herself off, Maria and Doris teach her to do the hora to "Hava Nagila," ("Let Us Rejoice"), Doris keeping her hand unattached to the others in an abundance of caution.

Maria invites Doris to come to the backyard where sunflowers, red yucca, and clumps of Dr. Seussian ornamental grasses are abundant. Offering the hammock to Doris, Maria sets herself up on a canvas chaise lounge. Doris longs to confess her desire to run away from West House, but she knows her explanation might make her look ungrateful, and she's unwilling to risk that. After she asks Maria to tell her more about her sister, and Doris expresses more condolences, she drifts off into a nap. She wakes refreshed, ready to face her family of friends again. Maria offers her a ride home, but Doris wants to be on her own. She'd like to hug Maria and Serena goodbye but settles for blowing kisses.

The Trump piñata is even bigger than it looks from the sidewalk, and the store accepts her credit card. She carries the piñata home on the bus, giving it its own seat, and nods to anyone eyeballing her.

After dinner, Tomás hangs the unfilled piñata from a tree. It's a treat enough to whack it with a broomstick until they're left with bits of cardboard and tissue paper.

Crammed together with Vihaan in bed in his white room, Doris confesses to him that she's afraid of being a caretaker again.

He is silent for a while, then says, "Maybe you'd have help, and maybe you'd know the ways in which you couldn't help. What are you most afraid of?"

She runs her mind over the losses she's had with her parents, with Howard, with her San Diego house devoured by fire. "Pain. I'm afraid of drying up and blowing away. I'm afraid, I'm afraid …" Whatever else she fears is just out of reach until she hits on it the way she connected, after numerous flailing attempts, the broomstick to the piñata. "I'm afraid you'll have to take care of me. That I'll have to have a caretaker."

"I can't say that would be easy," he says. "But it's not all about easy."

She thinks of Serena saying to Maria, "… you like people too much." That's what makes it hard.

Chapter 30: Recycle

The filling for the sinkhole is now deteriorating, wavy, pitted, and cracked where it had been level and smooth for a while. On their excursions, the roommates drive around it to avoid subjecting it to the Odyssey's weight. Tomás begins his series of phone calls to the city street repair department, knowing it might take a while to get someone to come look at it.

Barry, Pearl, and Jane have been sequestering in their rooms, having tested positive for COVID, but all fortunately have mild cases. Though he'd thought he might have allergies, Barry took a rapid test just in case, which led the rest of them to test. Sometimes there's a chorus of coughing from the various sick rooms, as if when one person starts, the others join by power of suggestion. Maeve whines at their doors, but they don't let her in just in case she can contract the virus from them.

The news announces the millionth death in the States from COVID, but the roommates don't discuss it because it's too depressing. Though not tragic, also dispiriting is the recent news that Medicare and Social Security might be reduced.

When the ill roommates are better and can breathe around the others without worry, they plan their annual celebration of the sinkhole repair and invite Cliff and David. As they've done for the past few years, instead of collecting compostables to toss into the sinkhole, they gather objects from around the house to donate to the thrift store whose proceeds pay for school lunches since the district no longer provides any for free. Cliff and David will contribute to the donations too, and when all of them are settled in lawn chairs encircling the patched-over sinkhole, they take turns saying goodbye to whatever they're donating.

"Amy's rings," Jane says. They're too small for all of the women except Ellen, and Ellen has politely said someone else would enjoy them more. They're gold and might fetch a good price at the thrift store, better than sitting in a box under Jane's bed.

Cliff says, "A fedora. I don't know why I thought for a moment that I was a hat person."

"Sterling silver candleholders," David says. "I polished them today for the first and last time. They belonged to my beloved aunt, but I have enough memories of her."

Pearl presents a pair of high heels.

"Those belong to you?" Vihaan asks, skeptical.

"Exactly. I bought these back in Flint in a trance, as if I were a different person with a different life. Cliff's not a hat person, and I'm not a heels person. I'm not sure why I moved them here."

Barry proposes they stop for a toast, and they pass around the Italian sodas and the ginger margaritas. Pearl whispers to herself, "To Ruby," and nods.

Vihaan has a stack of spotless white polo shirts. "I don't need fourteen shirts. Seven is more than enough."

Barry leaves for a moment, then he's dragging to the doorway a midcentury modern chair for which he paid way too much and that sits in the corner of his bedroom and functions as a place to drape clothes. "Too pretty and uncomfortable," he says, "like Pearl's heels."

Doris reveals a red lacquered box with red lacquered coasters inside. "This only has four," Doris says, "and, besides, we don't have any surfaces that require coasters." These had been a wedding gift from a coworker, another lifetime ago. She associates them with grabbing eye-candy objects randomly and needlessly to stuff into her car before she fled the San Diego wildfire. From a nearby street, a car backfires, and Doris starts, as she's been wont to do with loud noises since the school lockdown.

Tomato crostini and Swiss chard tartlets are the official dishes of the holiday (or hole-day, as they sometimes call it), and Barry passes around platters of each. Tomás shows them the dozen tiny moonlight towers he'll donate to the thrift store. Ellen's painted a couple of portraits of century plants in bloom, enjoying their combination of majesty and absurdity.

A few members of the semi-feral cat colony wind through the chairs, searching for crumbs. They seem unafraid of Maeve, who sniffs the air and wags her tail wildly but doesn't chase them. Then Maeve growls and whines at the patched-over sinkhole. Ginger's fur bushes out, and she arches her back.

David lies on the ground over the sinkhole, his ear to it. He'd been hoping to do a cartwheel instead. He might hear something, but he can't say for sure. The ground is warm on his cheek, lulling, but he springs up and brushes a pebble off his chin because he needs to be alert for his friends. In the morning, he'll call the city and try to get past the voicemail to a live person who can help before the sinkhole swallows up their street.

Acknowledgments

I'D LIKE TO thank those who've inspired and encouraged my writing and reading (apologies for the recency bias): agent/writer/teacher Madison Smartt Bell and editor/writer Bill Burleson; Helen Schulman and Bruce Handy; Martha Boethel; Amy Hufford; Judy Temple; Isabella Khavash; Celia Bell; Alan Greenberg and Deborah Beck; Mark Gozonsky and Stephanie Astrow; Karen Dominguez; Marilyn Rucker Norrod; Nancy Gore; the Austin Ladies' Penmanship Society; St. Lawrence University; the Iowa Writers' Workshop; and Barnard College. Thank you to the OG book club I joined in 1995, especially Rachel Jenkins. I also enjoy a neighborhood book club, spearheaded by Kerry Drake.

Speaking of neighbors, thank you to Cathy Savage and the Swole Patrol; Lori Nazareth, and her mindfulness/yoga group; and Sara Schaubert, who initiated the Empty Nesters.

Thank you to the University of Texas at Austin Master of Social Work program. As a psychotherapist for the past thirty-plus years, I've had the honor of making a meaningful living. Although I can't thank clients by name, you know who you are.

Friends and therapists, Martha Vogel, Sandra Grimes, and Anne Minor, thank you. I'm grateful to therapists Marcel Gamboa, Lee Land, and Debbie Guariguata for your guidance and care during my tough times.

Thanks for putting me on earth, Kuznets and Rostow families. From you I inherited my love of the arts, of cats, and of questions. Thanks to my favorite only sister, Naomi Kuznets, for walks and Twizzlers, and my favorite only nephew, Ben Kuznets-Speck, for allowing me to be "Aunta Mimi" and for making the world better. Thank you, Annie Villalobos and son Gabriel, for your lovely friendship with my original family. Thank you to Judy (Kuznets) Stein for your creativity. Thank you to the Taubs, the puzzle-loving family into which I married.

In memoriam, in chronological order: Mow-Mow, first love who purred; Eric Ashworth, my "boss" at Donadio's, the brother I'd wished I had, and his partner, Rick Kot (still going strong); my grandmother, Edith Kuznets, a dry wit and great storyteller who accepted me all ways and always; Jim Dowling, ethical and good-humored stepfather; Lois Kuznets Dowling, mother, literature professor, and my first love, who stood up for what she believed in and loved a good laugh; Benita Raphan, filmmaker extraordinaire; Alejandro Negro y Blanco Kuznets Taub, tuxedo with the mostest; my in-laws Phyllis Spinrad Taub, who inspired with her joie de vivre and Mel Taub, Brooklyn's foremost cruciverbalist; and Susann Rae Horton, adoptive auntie.

To my sweeties: best and only husband ever, Max, scientist and aspiring musician, you're such a swell companion on the lifeboat. Then we have climate scientist and mensch, Eli, my favorite and only child; you've helped me grow older and wiser. If our lives together were a well-written book, I've loved reading and rereading it, and I look forward to the sequel. Simone Noir de Beauvoir and Jean Jaques "J.J." Pretty Boy Rousseau, you're our Ginger and Fred.

If you're wondering why I failed to mention you here, it's just that I'm lucky to have known so many good eggs, and I've had to limit myself.

Flexible Press, thank you for donating 10 percent of profits from this book to World Central Kitchen. My character Barry experienced food insecurity as he grew up. We all should be well fed, and I'm rooting for humanitarianism.

ABOUT THE AUTHOR

UNLIKE THE CHARACTERS in *The Gray New Deal*, Miriam Kuznets has yet to live in a co-op, though she likes to imagine she could learn to play that well with others in tight quarters someday. She earned an MFA in fiction writing from the Iowa Writers' Workshop, and her fiction and nonfiction have appeared in *Narrative*, *Austin Noir*, *The Southern Review*, *The Antioch Review*, *Ascent*, and other publications. Barnard College and the Poets and Writers Exchange awarded her top prizes for fiction; she had a teaching residency at St. Lawrence University and a fiction residency at Yaddo. She lives in Austin with her husband, works as a psychotherapist, and enjoys visiting with her adult child.

www.ingramcontent.com/pod-product-compliance
Lightning Source LLC
LaVergne TN
LVHW041917070526
838199LV00051BA/2643